THE HOUSE
OF OTHERS

THE HOUSE
OF OTHERS

Silvio d'Arzo

Translated by
Keith Botsford

TMP

The Marlboro Press/Northwestern
Evanston, Illinois

The Marlboro Press/ Northwestern
Northwestern University Press
Evanston, Illinois 60208-4210

Printed in the United States of America

ISBN 0-8101-6000-5 (cloth)
ISBN 0-8101-6001-3 (paper)

Library of Congress Cataloging-in-Publication Data

D'Arzo, Silvio.
    [Casa d'altri. English]
    The house of others / Silvio d'Arzo ; translated by Keith
Botsford.
        p   cm.
    ISBN 0-8101-6000-5 (cloth : alk. paper).—ISBN 0-8101-6001-3
(pbk. : alk. paper)
    I. Botsford, Keith, 1928– . II. Title.
PQ4864.A78C3713 1995
853'.914—dc20   95-23486
                                                      CIP

The paper used in this publication meets the minimum
requirements of the American National Standard for Information
Sciences—Permanence of Paper for Printed Library Materials,
ANSI Z39.48-1984.

CONTENTS

INTRODUCTION

Silvio d'Arzo (Ezio Comparoni) 1920–52

I ask you . . . will the man who wrote this story, with its incongruities, its faults, its disproportions, one day be able to write something that is truly "his"?

—Silvio d'Arzo to Emilio Cecchi, 26 February 1946

Brief life, brief study. It's not always true: see Rimbaud. In the case of the singular Silvio d'Arzo, forget it. Here is a man who has only one work, the title story of this collection, that is at all read; a man who didn't quite make it to his thirty-second birthday and lived almost all his life in the provincial obscurity of Reggio Emilia; but a man so dedicated to literature that he managed to produce a fairly considerable oeuvre: a half-dozen novellas, a small but assured body of poetry, three remarkable fables for children, and a number of highly original literary essays (d'Arzo on Polonius, Henry James, or Conrad is a revelation).

What are we to make of him? Of his willful sorrow, his intransigent personality, the refinement of his style, his evasiveness toward the real world that he was just coming to grasp even as he was dying?

I have before me just about all of d'Arzo, a pile, say, four or five inches high. Alongside that pile are two thin notebooks containing nearly all the available critical writing on his work, mostly photocopied from Italian literary magazines or the "arts" sections of Italian newspapers, most dating back to the 1950s, in all totaling maybe fifty articles and fading fast. In English, nothing.

Everyone seems puzzled by him. D'Arzo had his own form of genius; he led a purely literary life (in a way that would be unimaginable now). Yet, curiously, nothing happened. His work had no echo.

Born three years before Italo Calvino, a writer whom he in many ways resembles (a similar taste for the fabular, a like concision and purity of style, an equal devotion to classical literature, and even a number of favorite writers in common, such as Robert Louis Stevenson), d'Arzo had a diametrically opposite fate. Calvino worked in the mainstream, aided and abetted by Elio Vittorini and Cesare Pavese; he was published by Einaudi; he was reviewed, and was himself a reviewer. D'Arzo lived in the dead end of Reggio Emilia, too shy, too melancholic to "connect," too self-absorbed to be readily accessible to a public that, during his lifetime, caught on to almost none of the undercurrent themes that gave Italian literature a European or international dimension in the immediate postwar period. Pavese (1908–50) and Vittorini (1908–66) are in the encyclopedias; d'Arzo and Fenoglio are not. Yet both Pavese's and Vittorini's fiction was published at the same time as d'Arzo's; so was their criticism; and their love of literature in English did not predate d'Arzo's. They all form part of a miraculous generation. If you need proof of neglect, however, just consider the tone of the letter quoted above, a letter written to a famous critic by a provincial nobody, the work in question being that indisputable masterpiece "Casa d'altri."

D'Arzo was unfortunate, then, in both time and place, which means that the critic writing today is faced with a double difficulty: he is writing of someone unknown and vanishing into the unread, and he is dealing with a body of work that could be viewed—and is so viewed by many, even friendly, critics—as incomplete. The main task is to answer that most difficult of all literary questions: does the work show achievement or merely promise?

If what we value in literature is a voice, a way of speaking about life and ideas and human relations quite distinguishable from anyone else's voice, then d'Arzo is a very remarkable writer indeed, informed by many (he obviously read voraciously) and indebted to none. Again, if we value originality, we should also value d'Arzo, for though his themes—solitude, alienation, a sense of "otherness"—are not unknown in European literature, his handling of them is almost unique in its fierce subjectivity and its absolute refusal to use *any* of the traditional, external trappings of fiction: plot, context, dialogue, analysis, development.

Let me first dispose of his brief and happy/unhappy stay among us.

Italy between 1920 and 1952 was hardly the sunny Italy of our minds. Reggio was a place of empty streets, few cars, and many bikes, of romantic novels sold door to door, of cheap rooms to let, of toy soldiers in shop windows, of 78-rpm records (which d'Arzo, with characteristic anthropomorphism, describes as "aware of new black shoes"). The first twenty-three years of d'Arzo's life were lived under Fascism, in Mussolini's curious blend of state socialism and would-be Roman triumphalism. The last seven years were shaped by a political crisis of left and right, barely resolved by the time of d'Arzo's death.

Of all of this, barely a trace in d'Arzo's work. The only evidence we have that he might have gone on to consider this atmosphere as a subject is the preface to the novel (or novels) he was projecting at his death: the vision suddenly broadens, and we hear of Egypt and Croatia, of newspapers and Marx. But it didn't happen. And in my view, brilliant as that preface is, the novel was not to be; and more's the shame.

His milieu (his own, and that of his subject) is principally, but not exclusively, one of the direst poverty. (When it is not, as in two remarkable stories in this collection, "The Old Couple" and "Elegy for Signora Nodier," d'Arzo well understands how the petit bourgeois protects the very means that he himself did not possess!) It is principally, but not exclusively, that of the two Emilias, the city of Reggio and its *retroterra*, its back country. (And when it is not, it is simply fabulous, invented.) Unless you yourself have explored these worlds, they are hard to imagine now; they were even harder to imagine in d'Arzo's day. Suffice it to say that when Zelinda, heroine of "The House of Others," compares her life, unfavorably, to that of her goat, she is speaking literally; and that for the city poor, the dark inner courtyard in which they hang their bicycles is the most that can be hoped for.

As for d'Arzo's race, it is that of the illegitimate. How he worshipped at the Tomb of the Unknown Father! And how difficult must life have been with his mother, Rosalinda—born in Ceretto d'Alba, extravagant, gypsylike, reading cards at a market stall, full of tales, insistent, possessive, determined, but all the young Ezio knew of family life and cohesion.

We know very little of his childhood, save what he tells us in a number of stories. There children—strangely like him, mesmerized by fantasy, by acrobats, by the past—figure prominently. As d'Arzo himself notes (he who wrote extensively for children), "We may not like ourselves; but we could never fail to love our own childhoods, and all that childhood means."

He seems to have made his friends in adolescence and young manhood. Precocious, his literary ambitions powerfully fostered by his mother, he is described as shut up within himself, unwilling to confide. He has complexes—his missing father, his poverty. Friends rarely, if ever, set foot in his home, though one friend bequeaths us a picture of mother and son in a kitchen that consists of no more than a table, two chairs, and a disorderly cupboard. We have one glimpse of him, at barely fifteen. He is about to publish his first book and the publisher sends his agent to meet the author. The agent duly inquires after the "Professor," only to be introduced to a boy shyly sitting in a corner of the room. He has blond, wavy hair and is dressed in a sailor suit. Giannino Degani, later his lawyer, meets him in the Prandi bookshop, where he has on the same sailor suit.

In 1931, having won prizes and scholarships, he enrolls in the Gymnasio-Liceo in Reggio. At thirteen he is reading D'Annunzio and Dostoevsky; in his next to last year, in 1936, he begins working with the admirable Giuseppe Zonta, teacher to a whole generation of young students of literature, who also gives him private lessons. No ordinary student this! He completes his baccalaureate as a day student at the Liceo in Pavia at sixteen and is already astonishingly well read. He is already familiar with the English and American classics; internal evidence suggests that he also knew German, or at least read E. T. A. Hoffmann, possibly Kleist, and, I would guess, Novalis. His frame of literary reference extends also to the French, for we know he read Stendhal, Proust (he must have read him in French or English, for Proust was not yet translated into Italian), Maupassant, and Villon.

D'Arzo obtained his degree from the University of Bologna at the ripe age of twenty-one with a thesis correcting Scheuermeier's data in the Italo-Swiss dialect map, specifically those relating to the dialects of Montericco and Albinea.

With his university studies completed, d'Arzo's life was normalized. He could now be employed and help his mother financially. He had already been teaching in Reggio while at the university and now took on classes in a girls' middle school and a vocational school. But a year later, in July 1942, he was called up for his military service. After a spell at Canzo di Como as a private soldier, he was enrolled in the officer cadets' school in Avellino from January to August 1943. About to be sent to the Aegean, he was in Barletta in Apulia when, on 8 September, the Fascist government fell. Like most of his regiment, d'Arzo was in the barracks waiting to ship out when he was taken prisoner by the Germans and destined for the camps in Germany. However, after a day and a night in the train taking him north, and while the train stood in open country, d'Arzo, together with another sub-lieutenant friend, escaped near Francavilla a Mare, where he hid with peasants until November.

From then on, the literary life—together with the "real" life that might have been, which was beginning to form in his mind—took over. The feeling of those times, minus politics, is beautifully reflected in the preface to *Our Monday*, the uncompleted work that would have marked his translation into reality, into the "big novel" he dreamed of writing.

The remainder of his life (he returned to teaching and writing) was much more straightforward. The army had opened him up (though it too was, as he noted, unreal), and he was known among his many friends in Reggio as cordial and open. He and his friends had their appointed places at the Caffè Italia. They sat there for hours among the packages of cigarettes and sugar or, if it was too late, on the steps of the Piazza del Monte under the statue of Boiardo, and when that monument was removed, on the steps of the Palazzo Bussetti. D'Arzo, clearly an affectionate teacher, often doted on his pupils (in addition to his regular teaching, he had a large number of private pupils). Very rarely did he leave his beloved city, except on long walks into the countryside at cockcrow, one or two visits to Rome, a prolonged stay in the Emilian Appenines collecting data on livestock, and a visit to Florence in 1947, during which he fell passionately in love with Masaccio and his *Adam and Eve*.

By the beginning of the 1950s, however, d'Arzo's cancer was beginning to tire him and necessitate ever more frequent stays in clinics. It was clearly not properly diagnosed. From the window of his clinic he could see the winter mist on the fields and in the distance the first hills, while nearby, at the Teatro Communale, there was a grand premiere of a recent American film. "If only I could go," he said to a friend, beseeching him to bring him every detail, "however unimportant," of the film and its audience. A few days later he died of a lymphogranuloma. As he was quickly spirited away (his bed was needed), his friends looked for his coffin in church after church. When they did find him, the only mourner present was his mother.

The rest of d'Arzo's life resides in his books. Here, too, there are difficulties. The chronology is not easy to fix, for much of his work was published only posthumously. We know that he was fifteen when his first book, *Maschere* (Masks), was published in 1935 (under the name Raffaele Comparoni). Subtitled *Tales from Town and Country*, it contained seven stories, largely based, or so conjecture has it, on stories his mother had told him. They are basically oral in nature. Like much of his later work, they derive from the street tradition of narrative, reports of the miraculous and the suffering; in mythical power, they are somewhat analogous to late-night talk shows and yellow-press journalism. That is, they are told from the impoverished margins of society.

Being the work of a teenager, they show their various influences (which run from De Amicis and Verga to Dostoevsky) and are consistent with his later work in that they contain tales of storytellers (or balladeers), bandits, beggars, and other semifantastical creatures who later reappear, most notably, in his books for children.

In the same year, La Quercia in Milan printed a modest collection of his early poems, *Luci e penombre* (Lights and shadows). These poems were not included in the "collected poems" published as part of *Nostro lunedì* (Our Monday), in 1960. The volume is exceedingly rare, and I have not been able to consult it. But the publication of two books (with whose money? how? were these publishers visionary, or did Rosalinda skimp and scrape to see her gifted son in print?) in one's fifteenth year can be seen either as remarkable literary precocity or ferocious literary ambition, self-knowledge, certainty. And how could it have been the latter when d'Arzo's most striking characteristic at the time was an almost impossible hesitation, an indecision about his own talent?

We must remember that we are dealing with a writer who published virtually nothing in book form in his lifetime: just these two juvenilia, one novella, *All'insegna del buon Corsiero* (At the sign of the noble steed), and an early version of "Casa d'altri" (The house of others), then known as "Io prete e la vecchia Zelinda" (I, priest, and old Zelinda).

It would seem that, by 1939, d'Arzo had already completed *Ragazzo in città* (City boy), parts of which were later used or adapted for *Esso pensano ad altro* (These think of something else). This title contains that important d'Arzian word *altro*, "other." This play on otherness, on being distant from oneself, on the double nature of being seen from within and without, persists in his private mythology as it does in Rimbaud's. One critic characterizes this early work as "pre-American": that is, as predating Italy's fascination with, and translations of, American literature. It was not until 1976 that Garzanti published it. This novella, which in its various versions seems to have shared space in his mind with at least two others, was rejected by publishers in 1942—not an especially favorable year in

Italy for so introspective a tale—along with *L'Osteria dei ricordi* (Memory Inn, as it is called on the manuscript sent to Vallechi in 1942, or, to borrow from Stephen Crane, Hotel de Dream) and a third novella written before he was twenty, *L'Uomo che camminava per le strade* (The man who walked the streets). *L'Osteria* was finally published in *Nostro lunedì* in 1960 by Vallecchi, and *L'Uomo*, of which the first eight of twenty-three chapters survive, was finally published in 1981 (in *Contributi*, vol. 9, by the A. Panizzi Library in Reggio Emilia), though a few chapters appeared as separate short stories in 1940 and 1941.

All of these works contain elements of the postwar d'Arzo; all are simultaneously derivative and highly original (it is possible for a true writer to go through phases of being influenced and yet remain very much himself); and all require the reader's full attention (something that is true of all d'Arzo's work). Ellipsis, the deliberate obliteration of the "landmarks" of fiction (such as plot or an intense, realistic context), elements of fantasy, require—and repay—close reading. You have to treat them as if you were reading early Kafka, like "The Aerodrome at Brescia" or *Amerika*, and seek in these transparent pieces of imaginative "reportage" the Kafka of *The Trial*.

L'Uomo che camminava per le strade and *Essi pensano ad altro* share an urban background, which both is and is not Bologna. The former is the story of Professor Carlo Stresa—a "moderate Mr. Bloom" in the words of A. Luce Lenzi, who edited the manuscript—and his accumulated peculiarities. Stresa wanders from one end of his street to the other and has his "opposite" (most of d'Arzo's work features incongruous, unrequited pairs and doubles), a Dr. Lada, blind and superior—the role played in *Essi pensano ad altro* by the drunken, truth-telling Piàdeni. Stresa's street, as one might expect from d'Arzo, is but a pretext for erring; it does not start at A and end at B. Instead, it is as interminable as the human histories it examines. The latter, which we know to be complete (we cannot be sure about the former, in spite of the fact that d'Arzo signed it at the end of the eighth chapter), is another singular work, based on the earlier *Ragazzo in città*. These two works, as well as the two that follow, can be considered part of one continuous work of literary exploration, which is self-referential, sinuous, and infinitely interconnected: characters, style, phrases, definitions recur again and again.

Essi pensano ad altro is a suffocating book that explores two sets of doubles living in the same wretched building: one consists of a boy, Riccardo, who has come to the big city to (perhaps) play the violin, and a friend of his father's, Arseni, with whom he lodges and who keeps and stuffs animals; the other consists of the protective Nemo (No One) and Enrico, an animal trainer and performer. There is a missing father (powerful and menacing) whose prospective visit to Riccardo looms throughout. He does come in the end, reeking of the country, when the animal trainer, himself threatened with failure, falls from their apartment into the courtyard and dies. There is also an unobtainable, matter-of-fact girl, Ernestina, who works in a stationery shop and whose fingers are stained with ink; and a mysterious Settembrini-like figure, Piàdeni, a drunk and a mystic, the purest of nihilists, for whom people "are born by mistake." Nemo and Enrico "have managed to discover each other and be together, and perhaps have lived only that they might discover each other and be together."

It's Beckett's bleakness, one would say, had d'Arzo read

Waiting for Godot, but d'Arzo hadn't. In d'Arzo, everything is amazement, what he calls the *dolce stupore di tutte le scoperte*, the "sweet amazement of all discoveries." Each character has his father/double; each is mysterious to himself and to his partner. *Essi pensano ad altro* is a work heavy with the presentiment of death, with that sense of the world being "provisional" of which d'Arzo speaks in his preface to *Nostro lunedì*.

All'insegna del buon Corsiero was d'Arzo's first emergence from within himself, if only into the eighteenth-century world of the commedia dell'arte. It was published by Vallechi in Florence in 1942 and had a modest critical success. Attilio Vallecchi (1880–1946), printer and publisher of the avant-garde paper *Lacerba* and a major backer of futurism, asked d'Arzo for a brief autobiography and a picture to use in promoting the book. The text d'Arzo supplied reads: "I was born in Fellettino (La Spezia) on January 5, 1917. I read classics and took my degree in law, after which I registered in the Faculty of Letters. I have been in Reggio for some time now—some three years. . . ." This dissimulation is accompanied by a picture (black tie, black suit, black plastered-down hair, radical white part, black mustache, heavy eyebrows) that looks like a cross between an Argentine tango dancer and a provincial bank clerk, as though the unknown and unrecognized bastard were invoking his own father as author of his oeuvre, aging him, thickening him, masculinizing him, offering this effigy as a form of propitiatory gesture: yes, you can take this author seriously. It is not *entirely* unlike the real d'Arzo (it seems to have been posed against the same wall as a picture taken in 1944, and carries the same intensity), but it is deliberately anonymous: not only unidentifiable, but also inscrutable.

The novella, set in mysterious, flat country in the Veneto, evokes the imaginative territory of Goldoni and the German Romantics. D'Arzo calls it *quest'avventura terrena d'altri tempi* ("this earthly tale from other days"), contrasting its real, human backdrop (an inn or posting house peopled with lackeys, scullery boys, cooks, maids, and an itinerant marchesa married to the doge's ambassador to the Porte) with the ill-defined supernaturalism of traveling comedians, a melancholy servant-poet, and its real hero, the tightrope walker, whose rope, strung across the main square, is cut by the jealous Lelio.

We know how d'Arzo felt about *All'insegna* and its near-contemporary, *L'Osteria*, from a 26 February 1946 letter to Emilio Cecchi in which he says, "A few years ago I wrote a poor little book for Vallecchi, and another had just been announced . . . but it was God's will that my eyes were sufficiently opened for me to prevent him from bringing out a second edition of the first or publishing the second." This self-deprecation is pure d'Arzo, but I don't think we need take it at face value: *All'insegna* and *L'Osteria* are the fables of a twenty-two-year-old steeped in Robert Louis Stevenson and the "angelism" of Zavattini, perhaps in Rilke and, before Rilke, in Kleist too.

The first is a tale of love gone sour, of a deeply concealed passion in a world where servants, the humble, are not "seen" in the external world and hardly exist save in their own emotions and imaginings. The tightrope walker, in his antique costume, with his certainties and his ambiguous smile, his intrusions into the real world (winning at dice, climbing up the ivy to state his exceptionality to the heroine, Lauretta), belongs to another world; he is seducer, enchanter, the Devil. The novella has its faults—its insistently circular style, clause within clause, its suffocating concentration on detail—but remains a remarkable, haunting fable in which he who dares falls and is killed but comes back to life and must, as the story ends, be chased away by those confined to the real world of kitchen and courtyard.

The second, *L'Osteria,* represents a step in a new direction. The "magical realism" that most critics associate with Gabriel García Marquez and the Latin American novel pervaded the Italian tradition in the years between the two wars. *L'Osteria,* in one sense, is a tale that takes place in Nowhere Land, and in a No-Time in which nothing happens. Its most puzzling aspect is its setting: a place called Sivilek, of which we know almost nothing except that it has a river and rain—constant rain—and an inn, where much of the "action" takes place. In such a place the real world (of poverty, of men for whom defeat and silence are natural conditions), a world that strongly recalls "Casa d'altri," combines with the fantastic so that the two are indistinguishable even to the protagonists: a widower, a barmaid whose breasts are "glory," a groom, the innkeeper, a smuggler, a little girl enjoined not to grow.

How did d'Arzo come to invent (and use elsewhere) names—Marek, Gonek, Rovan Giber, Lepic—that are vaguely Czech? We do not know, though we do know that part of his last, unfinished novel was to take place across the Adriatic, among Slavs.

The stylistic change is considerable. The key scenes, mysterious as they are, are now in dialogue. Italian critics take this to be the result of the influence of Ernest Hemingway; but, if so, d'Arzo chose a peculiar Hemingway as his model. It is a sign of his acute perception that d'Arzo's

Hemingway is very much his own, a man who, as he wrote in 1951, is "anything but primitive, or barbarous," whose sadness is that of an "exceedingly civilized man." Hemingway's dialogue, he argues, is one "whose repetitions and pauses produce ineffable meanings and resonances." It is easy, d'Arzo says, "to strike a flame: what is important (and difficult) is to leave no trace of sulphur." It is just this, I think, that d'Arzo was after, just this that he tried out in *L'Osteria* and brought to fruition in "Casa d'altri."

There is a passage in d'Arzo's wonderful letters to Ada Gorini (wonderful because they are the traces of an elusive and unconsummated passion) that illustrates his peculiar turn of mind. He had just sent her, his "double," Conrad's *Lord Jim*, whose protagonist is as passionate and vulnerable as himself. Now, he writes, "I'd like to tell you something."

The other day, you were talking about the song of a swan. And I tell you, swans sing, yes, but then they die: they don't accept being cooped up in a courtyard. For that end, there are ducks. And ducks are ducks. They do not sing. All they have is unending appetite. Nothing else. We spoke of ghosts: but ghosts don't cry, as you did: and they are lugubriously coherent: whereas you are a mass of magnificent incoherences. You're an incoherence dressed as a woman. You said, there is nothing nobler than suffering, and that may be so, but "wanting" suffering, "choosing suffering" is to flee real suffering: it is a highly refined form of egotism. You're wild; you seek a cage. You say you're weak, but you impose rules on yourself. You say the flesh does not exist, yet you make your spirit depend on the flesh. (19 May 1950)

No more and no less than his characters, d'Arzo is cooped up in his courtyard; he and his people are ducks who would be swans. To him, with his terrible, frustrated appetite, it is a thing of wonder that Ada Gorini's spirit depends on the flesh. He himself is a ghost, a fate he examines in his beautifully crafted essay on Henry James, for James's characters "have the discretion of ghosts; and some are as incorporeal as ghosts, and sometimes make even less noise, and especially love the shade. At first sight, they may seem more like presences than men." But, he goes on to say:

The most intimate and essential feature of ghosts, that most attractive or dismaying to us, is not their inconsistency or pallor (and even less their white sheet); what makes them both horrible and pathetic is their exile's condition, the way they are condemned to wander through places and memories that are not their own, their inability to communicate, their lack of roots, their eternal, absolute extraneousness: to everything and to all; and to themselves. Nothing is more casual, more gratuitous than a ghost: and, for this very reason, nothing is more monstrous. They have no history; thus no society. Their obtuse faithfulness to a given place is dictated by necessity . . . like that of a bat in his belfry. One can't even say they "are"; they merely exist.

James is not like that, and d'Arzo would like not to be like that.

D'Arzo explores this ghost theme, with its alienated survivors in the real world, in much of his fiction (in some ten stories, in particular, "Penny Whirton and His Mother") and criticism (now collected, except for his essays on Maupassant and Villon, in *Contea inglese* [Palermo: Sellerio, 1987]) written between 1949 and his death.

It is in this period that a new d'Arzo emerges, one whose preoccupations shift from irreality and fantasy to moral problems situated in a thoroughly real, if still somewhat mysterious and bleak, world. Chief of these many brilliant stories is "Casa d'altri," or "The House of Others." This long story was first published as "Io prete e la vecchia Zelinda," in *l'Illustrazione italiana* 29–30 (18 and 25 July 1948) under the name Sandro Nedi. In 1952, much reworked, with a different ending and a number of scenes excised for greater dramatic coherence and to bring out Zelinda's moral dilemma in its starkest form (Are there "exceptional" cases in which what is forbidden by the Church is licit? Can one, if one's life is worthless, put an end to it?), it was published in *Botteghe oscure* (no. 10). A year later, grossly traduced by the director Blasetti, it was one of eight stories filmed for *Tempi nostri Zibaldone II;* Sansoni published it in book form the same year. That was about as near as d'Arzo got to fame and its accompanying vulgarities.

An earlier English version entitled "Exile," translated by Bernard Wall, was published in *Encounter* no. 5 (1954) at the urging of Niccolò Chiaramonte, and was reprinted in *Stories of Modern Italy* (New York, 1960). This is a serviceable translation, but also one that Americanizes (in the wrong sense) and flattens out the elaborate comings and goings, the repetitions and echoes, in d'Arzo's style. None of the other four texts included in this volume—"Elegia alla Signora Nodier," first published in *Cronache* no. 3 (18 January 1947); "Due vecchi," likewise in *Cronache* nos. 29 and 30 (19 and 26 July 1947); "Un minuto così," in *Palatina* no. 6 (April–June 1958); and the preface to *Nostro lunedì,* in the volume of that name in 1960—has previously been translated into English.

If we had only "Casa d'altri" and d'Arzo's other late stories to remember him by, that would still be a great achievement. In my view, "Casa d'altri" is as near to "perfect" a story as it is possible to write. Why? First, because of its language, which is attenuated, transparent, subtly rhythmical, exquisitely poised (as Moravia pointed out) between the real and the poetic. Second, because of the subtlety of the characterizations: the priest with his doubts and Zelinda with hers, the pair of them locked together in an eternal and timeless conflict between what is and what should be. Then, because of its sense of the sacred, a factor that has all but disappeared in twentieth-century literature, its understanding that human beings operate under a divine providence or fatality and must measure themselves not just against each other but against Him. Because of its understanding of the enduring context of a mountain people who know themselves to be what they are, and who seek, in art (as in the age-old pageant treated in the story) and in the supernatural, some relief from the enforced ordinariness of their lives. And because the priest and Zelinda are deeply human and, as humans, are aware of each other in such startling, obsessive ways, yet are surrounded by the trivial details—whether of burials, pasturage, the weather, or cantankerous old ladies going on pilgrimage—that make up the very monotony of their lives, a depth plumbed elsewhere only by Joyce.

The other stories in this volume, with their attendant horrors when the real world reaches into private lives, are lesser only in scale. Full of ambiguities and ironies, they are rich in life reflected upon, absorbed, and re-created with special art. Not many writers are able to sum up, in as brief a space, a life such as that of the splendidly egotistical Signora Nodier, the mystery of her installation in the province, and her "solemn, yes, too solemn" general with

his love of hunting; or to provide a reversal half so sur-
prising as the revelation of the "young girl you once
taught to fish." What affection d'Arzo feels for the
Grimaldis in "Due vecchi," whose lives are changed radi-
cally by an importunate blackmailer (a semiliterary man).
He writes that while "great tragedies leave me indifferent,"
there are "certain subtle pains, some situations and relationships, that move me more than a city destroyed by
fire." In "Un minuto così," the latest of these stories, the
compression of much of postwar Italian history (the country's "Turkish times") into a single symbolic incident, the
finding of a belt buckle that leads to a grave ("the fact is,
these are curious times"), is even fiercer. There is, in the
mutual incomprehension of the guileful peasant Cloanti
and the schoolteacher who just wants "to live to be an old
man," a distillation of class warfare as suggestive as any to
be found in far more socially conscious and politically
"committed" novels.

As for the preface to *Nostro lunedì*, it is hard to think of
an opening chapter so rich in possibilities, or of a narrator
so scrupulously honest about himself and his past. We
know just a tantalizing bit about what the general line of
this novel was to be: a few notes and a few preliminary
stories. At d'Arzo's death, they were gathered together
under the general title *Senza bandiera* (Without a flag) or *Un
eroe dei nostri tempi* (A hero of our times)—a title significant-
ly lifted from Lermontov (Lermontov's "time" has become
d'Arzo's "times"). This can be no accident. Lermontov's
pre-existentialist novel, which has found a new audience
in our own times, has many affinities, both in style and
construction, with d'Arzo's. If you read "Our Monday, A
Preface," the last text in this volume, you will have an

answer to the question posed at the beginning. Here is both achievement—a new style, a new perception of reading, a new vigor—and promise. To quote Wystan Auden, with whom I was once discussing "major" and "minor" writers, "There are no major and minor writers, only different ones."

Poor d'Arzo. No one ever reimbursed him for his ticket to life. It is we who are the poorer for his premature death.

Keith Botsford
Boston, 1 May 1994

THE HOUSE
OF OTHERS

"So you can't get up there by train. . . ."

"Not by bus either. . . ."

". . ."

"It takes two or three hours on muleback. Not in winter, mind you. And not when the thaw comes."

"Then you couldn't do it in five even."

"Beh! . . . But I suppose it's got a name at least."

"Yes, I think so. It must be just about the only thing it does have."

I

Suddenly, from the path up to the pasture, but still some way off, came the sound of a dog barking.

We all lifted our heads.

Then two or three dogs. Then the sound of the little bronze goat bells.

By candlelight, I bent over the leaf mattress, I and two or three housewives, and, farther back, more old women from the village. Ever been to an anatomy lesson? Good. In a way that's how it was with us. Inside the reddish circle shed by the candle end all you could see was our six faces, linked to each other as if before the Chistmas crib, and that big pallet in the middle, a bit of wall blackened by smoke, and a beam even sootier. The rest was darkness.

Rising to my feet I said, "Did you ladies hear something?"

The oldest of the lot picked up the candle-stub and went over slowly to open the window. For a moment we were all in complete darkness.

The air around us was violet, and violet the paths, the

grass of the pastures, the folds and ravines of the mountains. In the middle of the shadows, far off, we saw four or five lanterns winding down toward the village.

"The men are coming down from the pastures," she murmured, rejoining us. "They'll be here in ten minutes."

That was a fact, so I breathed more freely. Words make me feel ashamed, that's the truth of the matter, and farewells have never been my style. Especially this kind. Furtively, without seeming to, I edged toward the door.

"So that's what we'll do, Father," a woman said, following me, "we'll wash and shave him, and they'll take care of dressing him tonight."

I said, "I'll send Melide to sew up the shroud tomorrow morning. And for the professional mourners . . . ?"

"They wanted three hundred and fifty, plus food and a night's lodging, so we'll do without. The more so because there might be relatives coming from Braino."

"That's right," I said, "it's probably not worth it, there should be plenty of people around tomorrow. He was in the May Day pageant too, wasn't he?"

"Yes, he played Jacob. And King Charles of France one time. Then, you know, after fifty years spent pasturing up in Bobbio, eventually everyone knows everyone else."

Sitting near the mattress was the widow. Tears don't come easy up here: she was as fixed and still as the old lady by the cathedral in town who sits there waiting for a few pennies. The grandchildren had been sent off to the stables.

"Good night," I said softly. "I'll be here tomorrow morning at seven."

She nodded. Two or three women walked me down.

Now you could hear dogs and little bronze bells more clearly, sometimes mingled with the sound of footsteps.

Behind a window a child coughed, and in the stables you
could hear mules' hooves and the jangling of metal bits. It
was getting cold. I crossed the stony little square and two
streets not much wider than an arm is long: so narrow, I
tell you, that a Falstaff like me has to sidle through, elbows
to his ribs.

From the pond I stopped to take a look downward:
seven houses. Seven huddled houses, that's it. And two
stony streets, a courtyard they call a square, a pond, a
stream, and mountains, as many as you could want.

The three old women stood there, motionless, on the
steps of their houses, under a lighted, open window.

"That's Montelice," I said to myself. "That's all there is
to it. All of it, and no one even knows it's here."

And I left by the upper road.

II

I barely shrugged.

I'm not saying it was a stupid question, as it might
have seemed at the moment; but any reply would have
been stupid.

The boy looked at me, waiting. Yes, he was probably
twenty. Perhaps not even that—eighteen. Eighteen.
Whatever, he was as old as he deserved to be; and apart
from his black cassock, nothing in the world was *newer*
than he was.

"What do people do, here in Montelice?" I repeated.
"*Beh*,"* I shrugged. "They live. There you have it. They live
and that's all there is to it, that's what I think."

Beh is the Italian verbal equivalent of a shrug, a sort of interjection, like
"well" or "uh," that frequently punctuates rural talk.—Trans.

My friend can't have felt very satisfied with my answer. He had caught me by surprise, sitting in my armchair without my shoes on, with my Falstaff face and body, and a bit somnolent on top of it all: and now, yes, that half-snoozing reply of mine.

Luckily he was somewhat educated and in a sense even rather distinguished—something new as new, as I said, freshly minted.

"Ah, I see," he had the presence of mind to say, as though I had given him some precise and confidential piece of information. "I understand perfectly. They live."

He was the new parish priest in Braino. Hardly arrived, he'd taken the trouble to come all the way up here to see me and get some advice. To get to know me, shall we say. Straight off he'd asked me about all sorts of things—dances, communists, morality, and so on—and, all things considered, had shown no marked desire to leave me at any time in the near future. He asked everything so politely, so casually, not making anything of it. Listening to him was fun. *Beh*, a bit sad, too. A bit. That little man over there—he works for the town, maybe he's a widower too—take a look at the suit he's wearing. What comes to mind is, it was once brand new. The little man, too, not just his suit.

"And then, they also die," I added.

Given my sixty years and those unlaced shoes down there, there was no risk that I might appear cynical.

"That's it. Nothing at all happens here. Nor in Braino. You'll see. Not in this whole area, right down to the valley. The men are away pasturing right now, and they won't come back before nightfall; someone may be out by the bogs cutting peat, and maybe there are women here and there gathering firewood. If you come across someone on the road, at most it'll be some old woman fanning up her stove. If you're lucky. . . . Or maybe a goat. Maybe just one goat. (In a way, the goats own this area; they stand in the doorways waiting to slip in, if there's a way.) And two weeks from now you won't even see that much. Winter comes early here, and it lasts nearly half the year."

He probably didn't credit me much and also looked down on me a bit, though charitably.

"I was referring to the people . . . the men," he said politely.

"Ah, people. It's the same with them. It's like the old story of the doctor sent up here. He arrives fresh as fresh with his Fiat 110 and his degree, and he thinks he's going to do God knows what: he kind of likes his martyrdom. For some people—for a while anyway, right?—martyrdom is not so unpleasant. On the spur of the moment he does the whole mountain on muleback, he goes into every stable, and everywhere else, too. Above all, to keep himself informed, he goes on subscribing to three or four journals."

I took another sip from my little glass of grappa. And he too put his to his lips—gingerly, hardly at all, like so, like a baby squirrel.

'Then he comes to see there's just arthritis: sciatica and arthritis, sciatica and arthritis, and nothing else. . . . So what's left to him? He prescribes iodine and puts on weight."

He responded simply, looking me in the eye.

"That's right, like me. Exactly."

"Please," he smiled, "that's not what I meant at all."

"*Beh*. It's perfectly understandable," I rejoined, I fear in somewhat too fatherly a fashion. But the boy wasn't the kind to accept easy gifts.

He got up with a smile.

"For sure, one has to look around," he said urbanely. "One has to find new ways. Every period has its own way, don't you think?"

He was right, I agree, and I could easily have said yes. The truth is, he was altogether too right, and for me that's more or less like being wrong, or worse. And then there were so many other factors. I replied in a completely different tone.

"Just one thing," I said. "Have you ever been in a mountain village, roughly like this one, for a month of constant rain?"

He looked at me, somewhat surprised. No more than that, anyway, I guess a little amused.

"With maybe two months of snow? Snow-snow, I mean. In no way like city snow or valley snow."

He waited to see what I was getting at.

"Well, I have. And for more than thirty years. More than thirty Christmases, you follow me?"

The man really had some tricks up his sleeve. He managed to look at me with both deference and diffidence. By now he thought of me as some curious sort of local fauna, basically not all that unpleasant—like the last of Garibaldi's Thousand, or the deaf old servant in town who's worked a hundred years for the same family.

"And what happens?" he asked, just for information.

"Nothing, as I told you. Absolutely nothing happens," I answered, trying to collect my thoughts. "It just snows and rains. It rains and snows, that's all there is to it."

I finally summoned up the courage to slip my shoes back on. My friend was tactful enough to turn away and stare down at his hat.

"As for the people," I concluded, "well, they stand around in the stables and watch the rain and snow. Like the goats and mules do. Just like."

We stopped for a moment by the door. There was something else he wanted to tell me. A goat poked its head in the door; it looked at us with a touch of disappointment and moved off, like a member of the family. To come back in a while.

"You see?" I said again, watching the goat. "Absolutely nothing. That's the way it is here."

"*Beh*, once in a while you meet up with someone. Like we've done," he let slip with a smile. "Up here, that's already something. Many thanks."

He went down in the direction of Braino. He turned left; he was thin and tall and dressed in brand-new clothes—yes, eighteen, obviously. There's nothing younger in the whole wide world. Or perhaps older.

III

It happened one night. At the end of October.

I was coming down from the bogs up-mountain. Neither glad nor sad. That was it. As usual. Without so much as a thought. It was late, it was cold, I was still on the road: I had to get home, that's all there was to it.

The shadows hadn't yet fallen: from just below the pastures you could hear the bells of sheep and goats. The very hour, you see, at which the sadness of living seems to come over you, along with the darkness, and you don't know who to blame. A bad time. A squirrel ran across the road, just about slipping between my feet.

Only then did I see, down there where the stream

flows some sixty feet below—doubled over, laundering
linen, old rags, or something of the kind—a woman a little older than myself. You know, sixty something.

In all that silence and that cold, that wanness and that
slightly tragic stillness, she was the only living thing. She
bent over, wearily I thought, and pushed her rags down
into the water, wrung them out, and beat them on a stone;
then immersed them, wrung them out, and beat them; and
so on, again. Neither slow nor hurried, and never raising
her head.

I stopped on the embankment to have a look at her. A
stone rolled down, right into the water, but the old
woman didn't even take that in. Only once did she stop:
she rested her hand on her hip and looked over at her little cart on the mudbank, and at her goat nibbling at the
grass; and then went back to work.

"Beh," I said to myself, "when it gets down to it, the
world can make itself a sorry place, can't it just? It's smart
enough for that; and no man could ever be so sorry, ever."

It was late. It was really late. Here and there you could
see the odd star. I carried on.

But the following night the same thing happened.
And another night after that, and another. At the same
hour, there she was, at the bottom of her ravine.

Neither sun nor moon, not a living soul anywhere
near; and the same little bells sounding in the depths of
the pastures farther up, the same stillness all around.

You're most welcome to laugh all you want, but even
the rocks at that hour were sad, and the grass, by then
near-violet, was even sadder. And there she was down
there, bent over the slabs of rock: she plunged her cloths
in the water, she wrung them out, she beat them, and then

again. Neither slowly nor fast, and without ever lifting up her head.

Easy to say, but you should have seen her.

"No," I said to myself, taking her in well, "I don't think I know her, not her; she's not from here, this old woman; she's no doubt a bird strayed from her nest. Anyway, it's best if it's she who comes to me. Sooner or later they all do, come to me. And besides, what could I tell her?"

Because by then I was a Sunday priest. I was a Sunday priest, and no better than that; no doubt about it. Good for a proper wedding and the catechism for the children, and to get seven goatherds to agree about a handkerchief of meadowland—you could do worse—and good for handling a husband who overdid it with his belt. By now that was my daily bread; other matters weren't for me.

All right. For five days in a row I saw her down there.

Funny people, aren't we?

Two steps from the edge of the stream, I hoped not to find her yet again. But the evening came when she changed from her usual position, and I couldn't see her any more, and I walked every which way, wanting to shout something or other at her.

IV

Another eight days went by; then ten. Autumn was in its death throes. Nights, the hedges frosted over, and the moon was colder than rock, still, round, and exact as it is only at Christmas. The two clouds that clung to it looked like air without light.

You went into the street at six and smelled nothing but polenta and chestnuts boiling in water. The little brass bells reached the village from a mile, two miles, or even farther away.

But the old woman was not to be seen.

I said to myself, "Sooner or later they all come to me. More so because winter's at the gates. They all come in the end, I know it, sooner or later. She too will have to come out of her lair."

It didn't turn out that way. Autumn went by. The hedges were no more than tangles of thorns; the men were finishing off the traps they would take up the mountain into the woods; and the old woman hadn't come out of her lair.

I did what I'd never done before. I decided to ask around about her. I gave a boy who occasionally served mass two rabbit pelts and had him cover the ground from the woods to the big folds and furrows on top. The lad made the rounds in all directions for two whole days, for he was in fact a good boy, full of ideas and devices, and, for a lad from up here, even somewhat educated: he went up the bogs and into the high pockets, the folds in the mountains and the pastures, and failed to find out much. I gave him a third skin, he went as far as the outskirts of Bobbio; and what there was to know, I got to know.

She lived alone, beyond the end of the trail with the oaks, right on the very edge of the parish, after which all you get is deep clefts with peat bogs and worse—if worse is possible. She'd come recently and without saying anything to anybody, arriving from those parts of Bobbio where four years before the Germans had burned even the stones; her name was Zelinda Icci, born Primo; she had turned sixty-three last August eighth, and now she washed her rags and tatters from morning to night for someone or

some enterprise in a village in the valley where a little
industry had sprung up.

Every evening at sunset, she climbed up the mountain
path with her rags, her little cart, and the goat (apparently
won in a village lottery); along the hedges she bent over
constantly to pick up dry twigs, or even just paper; and in
front of the little tabernacle with its Jesus she crossed herself and bowed her head. Never once had she taken part in
the procession, or come to vespers, or to church.

That sums up what I learned.

On the night of the ninth I was rehearsing a miracle
play with the boys. The door opened and Melide came in
with three or four goat cheeses. She had just come back
from sewing up a shroud for an old man. The bad time was
coming for the old. When their death agony began, they
always sent for her right away: she kept vigil for a night,
two, three; she washed the dead man and sewed up his
shroud; and every time she returned she always brought
something back.

"An old woman needs you. She's in your study."

"I know," I said, "I know." (Though I didn't, and it
turned out to be a lot more than I thought.) "I told her to
drop by."

"And now thank you and goodnight and sweet
dreams"—I wanted to sound cheerful—"and keep well
until tomorrow morning; but the fact is, my good people,
I don't need you any more this evening."

So they all left, and I remained alone in the rectory.

The hall was darker than an oven, and as I looked at
the little streak of light that sneaked from the crack in the
door, I felt like someone in debt: the man I owe money to
is out there waiting, and I have no idea what to do, for the

money I borrowed from him is long spent, all I have is a little change, and that's clutched in one hand.

This hadn't happened to me in centuries, and it made me think.

I heard the boys saying goodbye out in the street. A pebble bounced on the stones of the square. One door then another shut, and the one who lived up by the bogs just kept going, whistling.

And I thought, "My old woman's here."

After a while I opened the door. There she was.

V

It was the first time I'd been able to see her close up, and I took my time observing her.

Her skin was dark and rough, her hair bird-gray; she had big tough veins that stuck out even more than a man's. And if there's any way in which a plant may resemble a Christian soul, she was an old olive tree growing in a ditch. Seeing her like that, I thought that by now neither weariness nor boredom could get through to her: she allowed herself to go on living and that was that, that was all.

I waved her toward the chair. But she smiled a wild person's smile, then dropped her head somewhat and came closer to the desk.

"So . . . ," she began, a little hesitantly, "though to tell the truth you don't even know me. . . ."

"*Beh*," I interrupted her, smiling. "Lately we priests aren't in such good odor, I know. But we haven't quite reached that point yet."

I said it in a way as to make her understand that what anyone may know about another—name, address, occupation, and so on—I'd known about her for some time now. The rest I expected to find out from her.

Looking away, she corrected me. "I was saying that I've never been here before today."

"*Beh,* winter's at the door, and there's always a lot to be done; I imagine it's even worse for you people. . . . Who says you should come to the rectory? The important thing is not to forget the number. It can always come in handy, that's all."

"And I haven't lost it," she said after a while, smiling as though using my own words was akin to drinking out of my glass.

"And you did well. Better than well. I would like to hope that it could really come in handy."

But even then she couldn't make up her mind to talk. So, to get her to spill it I could think of no better way than to behave as though she weren't even there. On the desk was an almanac from five or six years ago, and I started to flip its pages and read it as though it were something really important.

This is how I saw matters. "Listen," I said to myself, "the old woman hasn't even begun to talk yet, and it may well be that she wants to be begged and begged, and yet still say no for a whole year. The longer it takes to say something, the more likely it is to be something important. The more it's a sign the question's an important one. I know that. And up to that point, I think I can cope. But what I really fear is that I'm no longer of any use in a case like this. This is a whole different language from mine . . . feast-days, baptisms, holy oil, a good wedding, by now that's my daily bread."

And I thought back to what I'd been twenty years ago,

when I read everything in sight, and into the bargain they called me "Doctor Ironicus" at the seminary.

"So, all I wanted to ask," she said, finally opening her mouth, "was . . ."

I looked at the almanac and said nothing. She too fell silent for a moment.

"Is it true or not that you. . . ? Yes, the Church . . . admits that two people who have been married can also separate, and one of them is free to marry whomever he wants?"

VI

A man could be angry for much less than this, for far less than this, as I well know; and so can a poor priest.

I put the almanac aside and looked her straight in the eye. The look on my face can't have pleased her greatly, for straightaway she began to fidget, studying her shoes, tugging at her apron and smoothing it down, and things even sillier than that, while at the same time withdrawing into herself, neither more nor less than a hedgehog does when touched. I'd spent days thinking of no one but her, every night I'd gone down to the stream, I'd had grand plans. And what did it come down to? The kind of story that would make the local stables laugh away the winter.

Wanting to sound ironical, I said, "*Beh*, as far as I can see, you've left the matter till a little late."

"That's not the question," she replied gently. "I just wanted to know if that's permissible in the Church. That's why I came, to you. For instance. . . ."

"You must be joking. The Church doesn't find it permissible at all," I broke in resentfully, "and if you must know, the Church is right."

"I know, I know perfectly well. The Church always says that. Every priest tells you the same thing. Including Bobbio's."

"Right. Of course."

"Right. It's right they should say so. You have to do that. It's your duty. I understand you pretty well, all of you."

"What's this *have* to? What is this thing we *have* to do? That's the way it is: it's like that, that's a fact. It's the Church that wants it that way, you understand? It has every reason in the world to want that, and it has said so for at least a thousand years. There isn't a bishop who could change a jot or tittle of it. Much less a priest."

She looked at me as one looks at a child.

Sweetly, she said, "I know that. I know it like I know other things. I was a Daughter of Mary some time ago. . . . That's not the point. I mean, I've been told that there are times, there are special cases . . . different cases, and then it's possible. You never speak of these special cases in your sermons (and I understand why you don't . . . I understand you perfectly), but still, there *are* special cases. People have told me so."

It was enough to make a man tear his hair out.

"*Beh*, yes, of course there are special cases," I had to grant. "Some very special cases. But very, very few, you understand? It's as though such special cases didn't exist. Maybe one in twenty thousand, or a hundred thousand, to put it generously; and maybe even fewer than that. And just imagine you've got one of the weirdest cases in the world, well, it's not weird enough, there's still something missing: that way you won't go wrong. And it's a great rule, that rule."

Sweet and implacable, she persisted: "But there are some. . . . You people never talk about them in your sermons, but nonetheless, there are special cases."

"Yes, yes. I told you that, Zelinda Icci, I told you. Very special cases. So special they might as well not exist."

"So there the rule doesn't apply. . . ."

"In those very special cases, obviously not."

She said, as if talking to herself, "So that it's really not a sin."

"So that it's really not a sin," I repeated.

Then something happened. My old woman glanced at the door and just sort of listened for a while. Yes. *Something* had to happen; something was in the air, I tell you. And suddenly, without knowing why, it was clearer than daylight to me that all her crazy questions about marriage and rules and special cases were just a pretext; and had I taken them seriously and lost my temper, well, so much the worse for me. To each his own, and so be it. That's when a priest retires.

"You see," she began, "in fact there's something else. . . . Let's admit that what I was saying was a sort of trick. I wanted to—"

Just then, out on the street, there was a sound of little bells and a rustle as of medicinal herbs, and of water taking over the road, and an infinity of gentle footsteps, and bleats. White shadows and dark shadows flitted outside the window. Watchdogs barked loudly, so she stopped in mid-sentence and listened to the noise and showed no sign of starting up again.

"We were saying, Zelinda . . . ?" I began without much hope.

"No. Some other time," she said hurriedly, as though begging my pardon. "It's too late now. Even the goatherds have come back, and soon it will be night. Another time, perhaps. I'll stop by and see you again. For sure."

I knew there was nothing left to do that evening: all I could do was stand up and walk her down to the church-yard. Now the moon had emerged, but it was so cold all around that even the moon seemed to shiver, the air was blue; and blue were the footpaths and grass of the pastures, the furrows of the hills and the dark stains of the woods.

I swear I was as sad as a little boy; and to let her go like that was more than I could allow.

"Hey, Zelinda," I shouted, "listen a moment. Stop."

Zelinda," I began when she was but a step away, "I want to be frank with you. You spend the whole day down there in the gorge doing laundry and washing old rags; you know no one, you don't stop to talk to anyone; and when it gets dark, you go straight home. But tonight, all of a sudden, you take it into your head to come and visit me, to walk two long kilometers in addition to the others you do every day, and then you ask me . . . you ask me what you asked me, that's all. All right, I've been a blacksmith, a doctor, and just about everything, and I no longer marvel at anything in the world. But all this seemed odd to me . . . honestly, very odd indeed."

Even now, she said not a word.

"Are you quite sure, Zelinda, that there's nothing you want to tell me?"

The old woman put off answering for a while.

"Yes, yes. . . ." she replied with some effort. "Good night."

"Good night," I said.

I leaned for a moment up against the apple tree in the yard and followed her with my eyes.

She walked off slowly, and with some effort too, I think, so that before she passed out of sight a fair amount of time must have gone by. Then suddenly she disappeared round the corner; and a little later, her shadow too. But the sound of her clogs reached me for some minutes more.

When I no longer heard anything at all, I went back into the rectory.

VII

Obviously, the old woman didn't show her face in church. Neither the next day nor any other.

And somehow I couldn't manage to find that spare half-hour to go down to the stream to seek her out. But you know what a mountain priest is like. There are months in the year—November, for instance—in which a smith is needed, or a doctor, but one of the freshly arrived sort, and a postman, and a barber, but the priest more or less has to cope all alone. And just then it happened to be November.

Now the curious aspect of the story is this: that every day I thought about her more and more, and at the same time I felt a certain kind of reticence and reserve, such as I hadn't felt for thirty years at least, and such delicacy that it was positively comical. But you just try and use a knife and fork up here, or speak decent Italian, or just offer your arm to a woman. Suddenly they all duck back into their shells. When you brush them with your elbow as you go by, the most they offer by way of acknowledgment is a nod of the head; forget about getting beyond that.

And even at that they would look at me suspiciously: as they would if they heard someone speak English. It was even worse in the confessional. I talked and talked, and then I had to stop and translate myself.

"But it's perfectly obvious," I said to myself while the boy took off first one shoe and then the other and I finally could sit down. "It's clearer than daylight. The question of marriage and all those other dime-a-dozen questions of hers don't interest her in the least. That's for sure. Only a poor devil like you, only a poor church-pageant-and-bingo priest like you could take her seriously for even a minute. Just think about it for a moment, if you still know how to think. A woman over sixty, doing what she does, spending every day down in the water washing old rags and tripe, and doing seven kilometers every day to take them down to the valley, and every day of the year the same, who has neither a dog nor a dead man, who says hello to no one and whom no one's interested in, you can understand she might have a few questions to ask. And it's understandable she might come and ask a fine fellow like you, the only man in the whole area dressed as you are, and who in addition has room and board with God. Anyone else would have caught on long ago. Think of the young priest in Braino, work it out!"

And the day after, thinking just the opposite.

"Very well, very well, we'll just leave the old mole alone from now on, dust her from your heart and don't give her another thought."

Then came that night.

It was dark and the moon was already up: the mountains, the hedges, the roads, and the tombstones in the cemetery (except for the woods, which were just dark stains) were brighter than the sun. It wasn't yet seven, and in every house some old woman was slicing up her polenta.

I thought I saw shadows behind the trellis of the old inn. They roamed watchfully amongst the already bare bushes: they were surely waiting for someone; and even a burglar caught in the rectory couldn't have looked quite as suspicious. Then, from up toward the pass, someone whistled in a strange way. Another shadow came pelting up and also vanished into the bushes. So they all hid.

I'm no nosier than anyone else, but more than once I'd stirred for less than this: a thief is a thief, and so are two thieves; but six or seven night-shadows lurking behind a bush gives you pause, and then, these are difficult times.

So I turned off the light, opened the window, and leaned on the sill.

A minute went by, then another. The moon, too, seemed to be watching. In that stillness you could hear the water and the creaking of a dead bough, and all those little sounds, so infinite in number no one knows what they are, and they just come from the very heart of the night and the mountain. A third minute passed laboriously. Then, abruptly, the sound of footsteps on the path. I rose on tiptoe and leaned out of the window a little. Where the path turns up the mountain appeared a goat, a little cart, and then an old woman.

Suddenly, there behind the trellis, six or seven boys leaped out with empty cans and lids, bits of corrugated iron, all the odds and ends left over from a village party. And three more from the hedge in front. Shouting and beating their bits and bobs of metal, they made a circle and danced. Then they all fell into procession behind her.

The goat was as if crazed: it kicked and butted and tried to gore; it tried to break free of its rope; now it dug in there in the middle of the road, now it gave a great leap forward. Without saying a word or even looking around, the old woman thought of nothing else but keeping up forward progress with her little cart, her bundles of rags, and everything else—no more than does a frog who thinks only of diving into a ditch.

I couldn't understand what was going on. I listened, watched, listened, but couldn't figure it out.

The boys were close to me now and I could make out their faces. Widower Sante's stepson showered her with a big handful of bits of paper cut up into confetti and began shouting something or other. I listened even more intently, but all that noise of pot lids and pieces of tin continued, and I could only make out a little.

"Confetti, confetti," they all shouted, laughing. "Hurrah for the bride! Confetti!"

And then all was clear.

"Ah yes," I thought. "I recognize the signature. Melide must be behind this. That night, she must have eavesdropped at the door, and she's worked it all out, so now she's laid on this little celebration."

Beh. Stupidities of this sort aren't that rare up here. Basically, they still belong to the forest. If someone's a little different from you, he gets on with his job and doesn't have a Christmas drink at the stall: first thing you know, before nightfall, this bunch will snip off his goat's beard.

Just the beard, of course.

But I was already thinking of the morrow.

I waited until they got a bit closer.

"Hey, boys!" I shouted when they were right under my window. "You fine fellows, hold on! Wait. The best's yet to come. Here's the bridegroom!"

And I pretended I was coming down. Down below there was a mad bustle and a crazy scampering between narrow streets and bushes, and lids of tin cans rolled all around. The company dispersed in an instant. Neither fast nor slowly, my old woman rounded the corner.

There was light. There was a wonderfully fresh and limpid light, and I could see everything: here and there, on her hair and shoulders, she still had bits of paper. All she had to do was shake her head a little and they would all have fallen off. Fine. But even that she wouldn't do. Not on your life. She ignored them, period. As she ignored me up there leaning out the window, watching her go by and then disappear.

The most absurd creature in the whole wide world.

"So, tomorrow, by the stream," I thought. "There'll never be a better opportunity. But that old lady will have to show her gratitude. Like it or not. Even a black would do no less."

After a while I could no longer hear her footsteps. A light went on. Down below flowed the deep water. The light went out.

Under the moon, everything now was clear and calm and fresh, right down to the bottom of the valley and beyond.

"Tomorrow, by the stream," I thought.

They say that such opportunities gladden boys and girls, both.

VIII

And so it was that the next day I dismissed my boys a half-hour early and walked down to the stream.

She was there.

I stopped on the muddy bank, right above her, some thirty feet up. Of course she'd seen me coming, at least since the bend in the road, but before she gave any sign that she knew I was there, she thought it a good idea to keep me in the waiting room for a fair while. I greeted her from up above by nodding my head; from down below, she did the same. No more than that, however. Just a nod. Then she went back to her washing.

That was all I got out of her, and there was no way to extract a thing more; so I had no choice but to take the road back home. And this went on for three or four days. Just the way I describe it.

It was enough to make you laugh.

"No hurry, no hurry," I said to myself. "Sunday comes on the seventh day. That's why it's called a feast-day."

Then one day something happened.

The rain had already begun. The smell of wet grass was everywhere. In the morning, the undergrowth in the woods was full of drowned birds; the water in the stream had risen six feet and many slabs of rock were already covered, vanished. To do her washing, she had to move some three hundred yards lower down toward the valley. For a moment, I couldn't see her, and I was on the point of turning back.

"So long as she doesn't take it into her head to provide more work for Melide," I said to myself.

A stone rolled down into the water, and I suddenly noticed her. She was there, hidden by bushes.

It was a real sign of understanding: a message according to the rules. And even now I can't imagine anyone claiming, in good conscience, to have received a note worth even a quarter of her message. My old woman had summoned me, that's the truth of the matter, and this time I also had the sense to understand that summonses of that kind don't require an answer.

My friends, never drink to the lees. I stayed there barely thirty seconds.

It was evening: the channels flowed hard down to the valley; the torrent carried away branches and occasional islands of mud.

I went home.

IX

To be brief, the days went by and she showed no sign at all of coming down from her branch. And it would always be that way. I decided to go up into her hideaway.

Meanwhile, I constantly studied the clouds and sniffed the smell of waterlogged roots to see if the weather was changing; and Melide watched everything I did. By then I was doing nothing else. And the skies did clear a little.

"All right," I said to myself that day—because before going anywhere I had to find a reason to do so, and to be the butt of laughter is no pleasure—"if your profession is to be interested in everyone, it begins by being interested in one particular person: just one person. But to be inter-

ested to the end, right to the root of things, there's no better way to take a serious interest in all those others. Otherwise, my fine friend, spare me the soft soap; the rest is
all talk."

Nothing to brag about, that's for sure; but I know
quite a few people who've stopped well short of even that.

By then it had stopped raining. The women had shift-
ed their cooking out onto the stoops of their houses;
chicks walked across the road, some of them even came
into the rectory. A bit of sun appeared in mid-morning,
but the color of old brass or fool's gold, not to be trusted
for long.

But here's the worst of it: after twelve days of rain, it
was also a day for visitors.

They started coming at around eight in the morning.

First came the six oldest shepherds in the village,
about their May pageant. No more *Jerusalem* this year.
Much less an *Orlando in Paris*. During the war their
broadswords had been handed over to the Germans, a
cuirass was missing—and more of the same. There was
neither money nor time. All right. Could I suggest some
other pageant in which these costumes weren't needed?
And which, above all, would be short? And contained
very few parts? One of the players had died in September—he'd played everything from King Charles to Judas
and was the best actor in the whole district—but he had
died in September. That was why the six of them had
come down from the peat bogs around Bobbio.

At the moment, I couldn't think of a single possible
play. I had other things on my mind just then.

"For sure," I said, to gain a moment's time, "*Jerusalem*
was just the thing for you." I looked up at the windows:

the sun was about to vanish; blue clouds buzzed around it.

I nodded. The sun had gone, that was that, and the room was getting darker than a cinema. The six old men were still waiting.

"Of course, it also had quite a few parts," I said distractedly. I continued to study the blue clouds. They could, after all, just blow away. A puff of wind would do it, or even less.

The six old men looked at each other.

"People came all the way from the valley, and even from the other side of the mountain," one of them said.

"And then you have to realize it's been five years since we had a May pageant up here," said the one who lived up by the bogs.

"I suppose it's understandable. . . . The war. . . . You know," I said, just to say something. A little light was coming into the room. Perhaps the sun would make it after all: all it needed was a puff of wind. I stretched out to look westward. "Why don't you try *The King of France?* It's pretty good."

There was a sort of faint confabulation: the six old men consulted among themselves in whispers, and then one of them spoke for the others.

"Yes, but what about the sabres? You want at least five, at the very least. And costumes and cuirasses. And how about women? There are three women in that pageant, and what's more, two of them have to be pretty young. Where are we going to find young ones now?"

I fell silent. So did they. They continued to look into each others' eyes; then, as one man, they all looked at the one who came from the bogs up by Bobbio.

"You see our problem, Father. We need something

short," the man from the Bobbio bogs explained patiently. "Something we can do with six or seven people, or fewer. And then we don't have any swords, that's a fact. And then there's the fact that Grisante died last September."

"Look," I said without thinking, "you suppose the weather will be all right?"

They all looked out the windows.

"We might have a Saint Martin's summer. There's always a week of good weather then."

"No. . . . I meant today. I wanted to know if we were going to get a fall storm."

My goatherds are now past seventy; they put on their saints' beards, their saints' faces; they each have two clear, bright-blue eyes; so that when they look straight at you, you always feel guilty. When the truth is they've got more lives than a cat and you can't hide a thing from them.

And they'd smelled a rat. Oh yes, they had. They wrapped themselves up in their cloaks and went away, peeved. It was the first time it's happened in thirty years, the first time since I climbed up the mountain here; and I didn't like it any better than they did.

From the window I could see them take the road up to the pastures. They went off in a row, up by the stream, and one after the other they took out from under their cloaks the cheeses they had brought for me. They climbed a fair bit higher and then they all huddled together. It was like a conspiracy. The one from the bogs of Bobbio was the first to set off again. They all held him back. They vanished to the left.

"That's not the way to the bogs," said Melide, nearby. "You take the right fork to go up to the bogs. That lot's not going home."

I turned and looked at her.

"They're going down to Braino," she insisted with a certain scorn. "Maybe they're going down to Braino to ask the advice of the priest down there."

This, too, was the first time in thirty years.

I avoided her remark. *"Beh,"* I said, "I never really liked goat's cheese."

She looked at me curiously.

"It smells of the wild," I said.

With two shirts on my back and a relatively fresh dog collar and a surplice worn only twice, if that, and more of the same, I finally managed to put together a pretty acceptable bundle; I stuck an ash pole through it and tried it over my shoulder.

At that moment, Melide came in and stood by the door. "Someone's looking for you," she said. I was more than a little embarrassed. Not that there was anything wrong in what I was doing, but certainly I looked a little ridiculous.

Downstairs, two leading Daughters of Mary from Grappada, down in the valley, were waiting. They had climbed up the mountain about a project older than I was: a pilgrimage to Oropa or Loreto, or perhaps both, a matter which (the fault is partly my own) had been endlessly postponed from year to year but now had to be faced. It had to be organized, they repeated without looking me in the eye, no way around it, you know that. . . . The money was already paid in. Well, not all of it: the people on my register, for instance, were missing. People were talking . . . nothing serious, just talk. . . . So far, at least. Did I get it? Did I understand?

They were, in truth, a curious pair. They kept their

eyes cast downward and their lips shut tight, as though they were offended by everything and everyone, and most of all by me. Two living reproaches. But I could think only of that bit of sun. Now it was there, then suddenly it vanished, and after a while it reappeared: as though dying, but hanging on just to please me.

I felt eighteen years old facing them. I just kept saying yes. Of course. It's perfectly understandable. It would happen this year, without a doubt, and in the circumstances I had even come up with an idea no worse than another.

Coldly, they let the matter drop.

"Yes, but about the servants?" they asked staidly.

I turned to look at them like one who's just woken up.

"The servants? Excuse me?"

They pursed their lips tighter.

Long-sufferingly, they deigned to say, "There was a question of whether all servants would be accepted, or only those with twenty years' service. . . ."

"Oh, I'd say all. . . . Yes, all. It's the best way, I think."

They consulted each other with their eyes. Under their noses flitted what for ladies of their kind might have been a conniving smile. I vaguely sensed the trap.

"Oh, it just might be, just might be," I said with an excess of deference, "though of course in that case you'd need at least three more buses. Perhaps even four. But if you can find them. . . . That is, if you're able to. . . ."

It was perfectly clear I couldn't provide them. And they knew it better than I. Thoroughly composed, they set to watching me in silence: to enjoy the effect. They looked as if they'd been stuffed.

"Then . . . then only those with thirty years' service. Yes, perhaps it's better that way. Just those."

They gave me a reproachful look: I was an imbecile. Then they looked at each other. The sun was out, and it was in; fresh clouds came off the mountain. I was beginning to feel terribly tired. I let myself slip down in my armchair with shameful placidity.

I tried to raise some sort of yawn. "Well, ladies," I said, "it's goodbye until Loreto or Oropa, maybe both. Put together some nice little trip, you understand. But right now I have a lot to do; and if you don't mind, I must get back into harness."

I knew I was throwing my hand in. But that way my two upright hens scuttled away. The last I saw of them was four ultrathin shinbones and two hats decked out with fruit made of cloth, and even the fruit looked offended.

Nor did this please me all that much.

"An odd day," I thought. "All in all, a peculiar day."

"What day is it today?" I asked Melide.

"Wednesday the sixth of November," she said.

Wednesday the sixth, eh? A very odd day. Different.

"It looks like we're losing customers," I said, trying to make a joke out of it. I had the tone right, but it was a little forced. Some things just don't give a whole lot of pleasure. No one's pleased by them.

Melide was on the point of saying something. She looked at my bundle and didn't say a word.

I slung it over my shoulder and went out.

X

So I left the houses and the pond behind me; then the inn, the cemetery, and the bog. Soon I was all alone, and all I saw around me were gorges and furrows, and farther up, a few pastures with, still farther up, the great wall of the mountains.

Two hours later I arrived at the split boulder where one night a shepherd was killed by seven brothers. A half-hour later, I had arrived.

The first thing I saw, about a hundred feet below me, was her goat, which was more than I'd expected when I started up.

It was already sunset; down in the depths the gorges looked like old rust, and the air was tending to blue; and anyone who didn't know Bobbio was still farther up would have thought himself at the world's end.

And there was my old woman.

She was sitting spinning wool on her doorstep, look-ing at neither spindle nor thread; and no doubt she had one thing on her mind, and only that one thing.

"Here's a proper meeting," I said to myself. "No one about, and it's supper time, and the silence must weigh on her too. Now she'll have to come down from her perch."

And I started down the slope toward her. But the old woman must have heard me. Without even looking up, she jumped to her feet and picked up basket and distaff, tugged at the rope of the goat, who was munching on thorns, and in no time at all the whole lot had vanished through the door. Between steps and door, nothing remained but a pair of clogs and myself, standing there looking at the clogs with my bundle, my stick, and every-thing else.

So far, I had no intention of making the trees round-about me laugh: all the more so because I sensed—yes, sensed—that just beyond the door, even now, she was lis-tening. So I simply walked off.

From the slopes of the mountain and pastures the blue of night was falling. There's no more mournful company at that hour. You're taken by surprise by certain kinds of thoughts, and memories surge within you. "Is this all there is to it?" you ask, like this man's no longer a man. Barely a half-hour passed when I heard the squeaking of a cart. Obviously the tailor. At that hour, and in that place, it couldn't be anyone else. He was heading home from his last trip before winter set in. I stopped and waited. It was him.

Because in his day he'd been in Savoy and had traveled here, there, and everywhere and did that sort of woman's work, he had the manners of a Frenchman and showered me with endless pretty compliments and kindnesses and *bonjours*. Finally he asked me if I'd like to ride down with him.

"Don't tempt me," I said.

He made a sort of semigentlemanly gesture.

"You'd be the first today," he said. "I haven't tempted a soul on this whole trip. Not one. Not even a woman."

"*Beh.* Perhaps first you ought to ask what your friend here thinks," I said, pointing to his mule.

Having a courteous word for all, he said, "Anointed flesh doesn't weigh a thing," and made room for me on his cart.

During the whole trip we didn't say a word. It was nighttime. You couldn't see a single house; our collars were soaked. Two widowers would have been cheerier than we were. I'd made a poor man's meal of my trip, and he'd had it almost worse than I.

"Not even half a suit," he said suddenly, a little sourly.

"I haven't sold so much as half a suit all day, and I went right up to the big ravines."

"They still have their uniforms," I said. "In winter they continue to get some use out of them."

"All right, all right," he said. "Just a manner of speaking. But you tell me why every one of them wastes a half-hour talking to me. That's what I'd like to know. Why ask me to spread out all my wares? Go to France or Savoy, you'll see."

He'd turned to look at me. He must have been really offended and he wanted a reply.

"I understand," I said wearily. "I hear what you're saying. But even that's a distraction for them. And they don't have many, that's a fact."

"And it's free besides. Great. I hadn't even thought of that. You have to admit, it's laughable." He put on a superior air.

"It's cold already," I said, trying to wind things up.

I could feel him watching me, even more attentively than earlier. He was studying me from a professional angle, you understand? For a while he was quiet. He looked and looked, and said nothing. "That crazy woman," I thought. "What a crazy woman!"

"You know something?" he said, nudging my elbow. "I know priests in the city who wear knickerbockers under their cassocks. Smart people, modern people. All the better: no one sees them."

He waited, smiling. I said nothing. "Did she come out and pick up her clogs?" I asked myself.

"For bike-riding, of course," he hastened to add. "And when you think about it, that's not so stupid. It must be a lot more comfortable, right? In addition to which, if they get called out at night. . . ."

"Yes, in the city there are some. It may well be there are some, in town."

He studied me again.

"Ah, but I think not only in town. Even up here in the mountains, I think."

"Am I wrong? Or have we arrived?" I wanted to get away.

With unexpected dignity, the little man pulled up on the bridle. He had suddenly become another person.

I got back home at ten.

I crossed the stones of the little square. My footsteps could be heard halfway to Bobbio. A watchdog barked in a stable.

I had only just walked into the rectory when the boy told me that during the afternoon the old woman had been by and left two candles and a letter; then she'd gone down to the stream, and subsequently returned to retrieve her letter.

"And there are your candles," interrupted Melide. She couldn't take her eyes off my bundle and stick. But now I was thinking about that letter and nothing else—about why she'd written it, and what on earth it had contained, and why she'd come and taken it back. And even supposing I was barefoot, I'd hardly have noticed.

XI

I was, however, to run into her some little while later. One night.

It had rained all day, rained as it only can up our way.

Not a single shepherd had felt up to going out, and all of them were indoors, caning chairs or making baskets or traps to set out in the woods. The ditches were full of gray water; the channel was in full flood, and from broken gutters the water spurted in big gouts; from the little square down to the valley there wasn't a hen, a dog, or a mole out.

I opened the window that gave on the plain. Ribbons of rain and the smell of wet grass invaded the whole room.

"No, no. You can't call this a good day for *her*," I said, suddenly shutting the window. "And tomorrow will be even worse, and so on for another three months at least. And unless she has a fat pile of letters to send me and take back again, I think the old woman's going to have anything but a happy time of it."

And so it went on all day. Then, when the first shadows fell, it stopped; and when the lanterns were lit in the stables, the moon also rose. Not round as in August, of course, but craftier, and clearer and fresher, as though it had been taken out of a bucket; and all the mountains, with their peaks dusted white, the pastures, the graveyard, the woods, and on the opposite side, the valley, opened up for me in a way that made them bigger than ever; all young and blue, with here and there touches of silver.

There was a shot from down below; and, after a while, two more shots. In ever-widening echoes the sound spread up the whole slope. Very slowly the sound died out toward the valley.

It was three or four years since anything like that had happened: the war had been over for a good while now. The whole village woke up. From all sides you could hear the kicking and braying of mules, the crying of children woken up from a sound sleep, people climbing out of bed and listening out their doors. But nobody unbolted, ventured out into the street, or shouted from the window to ask what was going on.

Still only half-dressed, I too couldn't make up my mind whether to go out or not. I went from bed to door, then back to bed. I stopped in between and tried to get into my shoes.

A little time went by. Probably quite a bit. I finally got one shoe on, then the other. I went out onto the street to have a look.

Not a single door was shut. The light from the lanterns hung from the beams spilled out to the middle of the road. A few women, half-dressed and with their youngest child in their arms, appeared here and there above the doorways; one threw an empty pillowcase to her husband below, and then a second. Without even stopping, a boy tied up his trousers with a halter and ran off up the upper road. Everyone had a pot or a pail, and the children each had a beret or two.

"Hey there, my friends, wait a moment. What's going on?" I asked from my doorway.

Those people took off. And the old men; and finally an old lady alone; a whole family, father, mother, and child; as on the last night of the siege of Troy. I couldn't understand. Then my altar boy came running up all in a lather, and at that point everything fell into place.

Four mules carrying flour had been winding down from the pass through the sour-oak wood. But there had been no moon then, and a wood is a wood, and night is night. The *carabinieri* had started shooting. So two mules had stampeded and taken off between the gulleys of mud and the bogs: and now, somewhere around there, there were six sacks of flour, or even more, scattered on the ground. Everyone was running to get a share.

"Hurry up!" the silly boy said before running off again. "They're picking stuff up with spoons by now."

"Right," I said. "Why not? When it rains, it also rains for me."

And a short while later I was off. But clearly I had something else on my mind.

There was practically no one left on the road and people were bolting up their houses again. The candles went out one by one. By the time I got to the mountain road, my hopes were just a wisp.

Instead, when I reached a dead ash tree, I saw my old woman with her skirts up, just like the rest. She was all but hidden in the deep shade that cut the path in two. I joined her immediately.

"Well, here you are," I said banteringly. "You didn't come and ask me for a ruling on this, did you? You know the rules for this, I guess."

I pointed to the flour. My old woman withdrew deeper into the darkness. She was more frightened than a mouse.

"No, no, I'm just joking. Wait," I said, taking her by the elbow, "all I came here for is to get *my* letter."

XII

As ill luck would have it, we had arrived at the hedge by her house, and all I could hope for from an old lady of her kind was the prescribed sort of greeting and then just to be left out there on the road.

" . . . so I want to thank you," she said, just as I'd foreseen. "And forgive me for the time and trouble. And good night to you, too."

"Good night? You're joking," I replied cheerily. "As for the trouble, there's no way I'll forgive you. Too easy. I've come to get the letter. *My* letter, do I make myself plain, Zelinda? Because, if you must know, the letter was already mine, no more or less mine than my books and my table, and any city lawyer or magistrate would agree with me."

She continued to look at me from a couple of steps away, her head slightly lowered.

"You're right," she finally decided, looking down at the ground. "I know you're right. But I think I too am right. . . . Well. The way it is with me, I think of one thing and nothing else for three or four days; then I go down to the valley and buy salt, paper, and ink; and then I send you a letter containing the whole business. And that way it's all done and over with. But it happens that when I go back down into the water, I think about it some more, and I see the letter can't help in any way, and I come back up and take the letter back. And the first thing I do is throw it in the water."

"But what *business* did you think about? What was it, this business? It's nighttime now, Zelinda, and there's no one here but us; both of us already have one foot in the grave; and for that reason I think we can talk about certain things now."

She lingered over that a second or two.

"What business was I thinking of by the stream? You'll be mad at me, I know."

I gave a faint shrug.

"You don't believe that, Zelinda."

"I thought that there are some things you people don't

understand. Neither you nor anyone else. The difference is, the others don't get angry."

"That too might be so. Who denies it?" I tried to maintain my smile. "Some things one does come to understand, others never. No more than a doctor does, who's spent years studying medicine and even Latin: then he comes up against a patient for whom he can do nothing, all he can do is sit on his chair and watch his patient slip out of his hands. Yet it's a good idea to call the doctor," I said, happy with my Sunday sermon analogy. "Everyone goes to the doctor."

"Not I," she answered gently. "I've never been. Even when the coal man's mule kicked me in the back I didn't go to a doctor. I just put some nettle leaves on it."

That was no reason, obviously. But I was going to have to content myself with that; and anyway, one had to take the good with the bad.

I replied: "But you did write the letter. And that night you came by my house. You came to see the doctor. . . . Say what you will, Zelinda, but it's a sign that this time you didn't find the nettles you needed. Well, what I wanted to tell you is this: two people are more likely to find them than one. That's all."

This time it was clear I'd scored a bull's-eye, for the old woman made no reply.

Just then, on the upper road, among the hedges and escarpments all around us, the gulleys and the pastures were all silent; the birds were asleep, so were the frogs and all living creatures.

In fact, after a while, she made up her mind.

"To get up every morning at five and go down into the valley to fetch rags, to stop in the grass of a ditch for a little while at noon and eat a piece of bread with oil, and then come up the mountain again to fetch the cart and come down to the stream to do the washing; to do this until six or seven, and Mondays until nine at night; and then load up the cart and go home, just in time to eat another piece of bread and oil, and maybe a few greens; and then to go to sleep. . . ."

She was breathing with effort. You could see that she was a painful burden to herself.

"And the same thing the next day, and the next, and all the days there are in the world—because this I know, this I know well—every day; and about that not even you people can say the contrary. . . ."

She stopped to draw breath; never in her life had she put so many words together. And I kept staring, and staring, saying nothing.

"I have a goat I always take with me: and my life is exactly like its life. It comes down into the valley, it goes back up at noon, it stops by the ditch with me, and then I take it down to the watercourse, and when I go to sleep, it also goes to sleep. Nor is there that much difference in what we eat, because it eats grass and I eat greens and lettuce, and the only difference between us is that I eat bread. And then there'll be times when I won't even be able to eat that. Like me . . . like me. Here's the life I lead: a goat-life. A goat-life and nothing else."

Bitter words: and I thought I ought at least to say something. I got up and moved a little closer.

"And that's what you put in your letter, Zelinda?"

"No," she said. And from her that surprised me. "No. Everyone knows that. Anyone who goes by sees that, and there's no need to say it."

Over and above that, I was beginning to disappoint her. Right.

"That wasn't what you wrote? Then what was it? Now you've extended your finger to me, Zelinda, give me your hand, for I'm ready to extend mine."

"No, no," she said hesitantly. "You people can't understand. I was with the Servants of Mary, I've been on pilgrimage to Loreto, on foot; I've done what God says to do, and no one can speak ill of me. I've never done anything really bad. And I thought that now God could do me some small favor in return, because I've never asked Him for anything. In sixty-three years I've never bothered him. And I've never been angry with Him; not once. But a small favor He might do me. There, that's all."

Once again she stopped, for now she was genuinely moved; and I continued to watch her and say nothing.

"That's why I came to see you that night: to find out if you people, the Church, don't sometimes bend the rules; and that business about marrying again was just a trick. All night I was ashamed of myself."

Again she stopped. I looked down at my shoes and kept silent. A minute, perhaps two minutes went by.

"So you want to know what I wrote?"

I limited myself to nodding my head.

"All right," she said. "I'll tell you. But turn around and stop looking at my face."

And I did as she asked. I assure you, I turned my face to the wall, like someone getting undressed. It never crossed my mind that anyone looking on would have laughed at my doing so.

Anyway, it was her business.

XIII

"In the letter I said I understood perfectly well what you priests say, because woe betide if things weren't that way, and who knows where the world would end up. I understood that all by myself. But as mine was a special case. . . . No, no. Don't turn around. You promised. . . . As mine was a special case, completely different from anyone else's, and I knew it would always be that way, and it could only get worse day by day—because I know that, I truly know that, it's the only thing I know really well . . . don't turn around. Please. Just face the wall. . . . So, without disrespect to anyone, I asked. . . . No, I know perfectly well already what you people would answer."

"Without disrespect. . . ."

"Right. In the letter I asked whether, in certain special cases, completely different cases, without disrespect to anyone, one might not be allowed to finish up a little sooner."

I turned around without having understood properly.

"Yes, even take one's own life. . . . Yes. . . ," she explained with all the tranquillity of a little girl.

And she began to stare down at her clogs.

I was so taken aback that just then I could think of nothing to say. Not a solitary word. But then that isn't quite true either. Recommendations and advice poured from my lips: "For God's sake" and "How can you say such a thing?" Sermons and whole pages, you name it. But they were all other peoples' words—old things—and they'd been used thousands of times before. Of my own, not a syllable; and this was where something new, and something that was mine, was needed. The rest was less than nothing.

"Well," she said after a while, "I knew that's the way you'd be."

The worst was that for a minute or more she continued to sit there attentively; she was still hoping for something from me.

"I knew that's the way you'd be," she repeated, hardly changing her tone. "I've always known. From the very first."

"Zelinda. . . ," I began, but so clumsily I was ashamed of all the words there are in the world.

"So why did you want to know what I asked," she said reproachfully. "You wanted to know, and now you behave like this."

She got up and vanished into the house. And I stayed there on the upper road.

Funny thoughts come into your head sometimes.

I looked around me. The dead season was upon us— the dead thorn bushes, the birds killed by the cold, night falling at six, the ditches frozen over, the old dying, one after the other, with Melide sewing them into their shrouds and myself bearing them to the graveyard on the hill, and the children confined to the stables for months to be kept warm by the breathing of mules. . . . A winter lasting five or six months. And what could this old woman have done about it?

I felt winter in my bones. I looked up at the clouds. They were bigger than a whole field. Then I walked down to the rectory, with the clouds following right behind me, as if they knew something. Funny thoughts come into your head, sometimes.

You tell me. What else could I have done?

XIV

By December, the paths up here are frozen hard, and you can hear a footstep from a long way off, all the way up from the valley.

With my head resting against the window that looks out on the mountains, I had been waiting for more than an hour. By then the air was the color of dirty snow, and the houses were paler and colder than rocks. There was nobody on the road. A boy with rags wrapped around his throat squashed his nose up against the window. A shower of gravel rattled against the glass, and only then did I snap to.

"The six old women from Bobbio," the boy shouted breathlessly from below. "I accompanied them as far as the bog. They should be here in half an hour."

It was true. Up toward the bog, right in the middle of the frosty path, there seemed to be something black.

The boy came up. He was no prodigy, didn't recite poetry or anything like that, but in his own way he was capable of understanding something of how I felt, because when he came in, he gave me the sort of look you give someone with an incurable illness. The boy was embarrassed, and he walked about on tiptoe.

We didn't say a word to one another. The windows too had turned the color of dirty snow. The boy with the rags around his neck was just where he had been before. From a window came a column of smoke.

"Should I go and get into my vestments?" the boy asked in a low voice.

"Not yet," I said. "It's early yet."

He fell silent.

Then he said, reluctantly, "Melide's already done her hair and washed her."

I looked down the road toward the bog. In all that white and cold, something black was moving our way.

"She'll be sewing up the shroud now," he said after a while.

"It's still early," I said with an effort. "And then we've got to wait until the mourners come. Did they accept three hundred and fifty?"

"Yes, three hundred and fifty. Plus something to eat and a place to sleep tonight. They say they've done seven kilometers."

"Then that's fair."

The room was dark by now; the boy was only two steps away, but he was no more than an even darker stain.

"Shall I go fetch a light?" he asked.

"It doesn't matter. Don't bother," I answered.

We were quiet now for four or five minutes. Then I felt sorry for him. More than anything else I wanted to be alone.

"Right, I think it's time now," I said. "Prepare my surplice, the aspergillums, and so on. And then get dressed yourself."

Off he went on tiptoe. But at the door he turned back.

"The old women from Bobbio also gave me to understand they'd like something hot. They say the roads are frozen."

I nodded. Fair enough. That too was fair. The boy went off.

For three months I'd gone down to the stream every day, and every evening I'd found her there with her rags. Her goat browsed nearby. I would stop there on the clay bank, as though by chance, and never for more than a minute, just long enough for her to note I was there and acknowledge the fact. And then I went back to the rectory. Not once in three months had she given me the slightest sign, or even raised her head. She was still *there:* that's all there was to it; and from the clay bank I could see she was still there; and about the rest I had nothing to say. And both of us knew we'd never speak another word to each other, not even to greet each other if we met by chance; and even that didn't matter.

And now it was all over. Something had happened, once, and now it was all over.

I felt no pain, however; no remorse, or melancholy, or anything like that. I just felt a great void within me, as though nothing could ever happen to me again. Nothing until the end of the world.

I walked up and down in the room where she had first spoken to me so rashly; I turned over a few leaves of a book and turned them back over again, or I drummed my fingers on a window: a mere child could have led me away by the hand. An absurd old woman, an absurd priest; an absurd two-bit story.

A noise rose from the alleyway below. The six old women from Bobbio were arriving. The hedges were all frozen. The six old women stamped their frozen feet. From another house rose a column of smoke.

The boy climbed up and knocked on the door.

"Father," he said without coming in, "I'll ring the bell. Melide's just finished."

"I'm coming," I said.

It was cold. December is a cold month up here.

XV

And here I am.

The old woman is dead. Melide's dead. The boy takes goats up the mountain.

Only once have I seen the curate from Braino. He was hurrying down to the valley. I was coming up the road through the pastures.

"Anything new in Montelice?" he shouted with a laugh from down below.

I spread my arms.

"N.N." Which is how the missal names the dead. Nothing.

He had put on too much weight for me to mention it, and he was still laughing when he continued on his way. He really had put on weight.

Up here there comes a certain hour of the day. The deep gulleys, the woods, the footpaths, the pastures—all take on the color of old rust, then turn blue, then violet. As the first darkness falls, the women blow on their fires, and the little brass bells sound clearly all the way down to the village. The goats come to the doorways with eyes like ours.

Then, ever more often, I think it's time I packed my bags and went home without a fuss. I think I even have the ticket.

All this is pretty monotonous, isn't it?

ELEGY FOR
SIGNORA NODIER

It is said that, for a certain period at least, we live a life that is not properly our own; then, suddenly, "our day" dawns, as might a rebirth, and only then does each of us have his own, unconfoundable life.

I have managed to observe this in more than one person. However, in the case of Signora Nodier, who owns the land next to ours, it seems to me that she always lived her own life.

An unusual case, Signora Nodier had got to the age of twenty-five, to thirty, and beyond without marrying; furthermore, no one had so much as made an offer. This despite the fact that she was distinguished and something like rich, owning land here and there throughout the province. Those who knew her when she was young still remember her expression as tending toward being beautiful, though not quite attaining beauty—and that is the only way to be seriously beautiful, and forever. To sum up, they found her disdainful. But no one was brave enough to admit it. It was a lot easier to say that she lacked "femininity" or "vivacity," the latter, and other such sorry tags, being the word most commonly used.

As is the way in the provinces, when she reached thirty people ceased talking about her; that lasted for five or six years. But just as she was about to reach the age at which it is vaguely said of distinguished ladies who have contacts and come from a wealthy family that they "do good works," the city suddenly learned that she was to marry General B. D.

At the time, this seemed odd (for in the provinces even the most obvious things seem strange), though in truth no one managed to explain why. When, however, a little later, they managed to get to know the general, seeing him at meals or out hunting, it finally came to people that if she had behaved in that way for years, defying the world with invariable calm, scorn, irony, and shadowy suggestions of a presumably unhappy future, it was with the certainty that what had now happened would happen.

Initially, the general was a disappointment. Then, suddenly, everyone found him to be elegant—slightly conventional, but elegant—and discovered that his elegance lay precisely in the fact that it had been noted only by chance, and after some time. From that point on, little by little it came to be acknowledged that he was a man of spirit and wit. "Ah, but he's a man of spirit. . . . But he has wit, let's face it," they found themselves saying, as though they'd been contradicted or the matter was particularly important.

If the truth be told, the general's looks and manners had nothing of the soldier in them: his bearing was as unmilitary as one might reasonably be asked to put up with. He had been about in the world, and his assignments had been vaguely bureaucratic and political; he had taken part in campaigns only rarely and at a distance; no victory bore his name. On the other hand, he had never committed any errors or stupidities; he had never been the object of ridicule. That dispassionate irony with which he viewed his career and, at heart, all his actions, had always kept him from disaster. Be all that as it may, military figures—some of them celebrated, with names that appeared in the newspapers—often sought his advice.

He arrived among us at the beginning of October. And for a few days, like some discreet tourist, he seemed to be everywhere, with a Scottie by his side. She was often absent. But no one noted how this absence was, in its own way, a reinforcement of her presence. Then one afternoon she was seen by someone or other hunting in the neighborhood, dressed in fustian olive-brown and reddish riding boots; and the little Scottie dog was always by her side.

By the end of the month the marriage ceremony took place and we never saw her again.

As I found out later (and I confess I did everything in my power not to lose them from sight for too long), they had gone to live in an old country house of his to which, during the hunting season, he had long been accustomed to retire. But we heard nothing more about them. For that matter, even the locals seemed not to have had much to say—admitting, that is, that the locals could find much to interest them in a couple so reasonable, so self-contained, and so little given to extravagance. Only a diary might have had something to say. But diaries, in which the gaps speak louder than words, are getting rarer and rarer; and in those days, I'd be willing to swear that Signora Nodier had not yet thought of keeping one.

Every morning he went off hunting; and every morning, from the drawing-room window, she watched him disappear into the fields along with the little Scottie dog. Occasionally, she would open the window to call him back and remind him of something. On other occasions, when he had forgotten something, for instance, his knife—which happened not infrequently—she would hold up the missing object, waving her arms, and the dog would run up and carry it off in its mouth. Anyway, nothing more exciting than that happened; for such appearances, and no more, were what the servants and the gardeners could observe on any day of the week.

Later, I also found out that the pair of them never made plans of any sort for the future, and often asked themselves what the next day would bring. In the autumn, the mist rose early on the river. Along the country roads, already hard with frost, there was no one to be seen. Sometimes the only sign of life was the flight of a wild duck; or else, at dusk, a child lazily wending his way home with a goat. It was therefore natural that in the late afternoon or evening their conversations were prolonged and frequent. But all those conversations bore upon the past. She could only feel truly sure of him when she had succeeded in conquering the entirety of his past.

Once, when suddenly they had almost been without light due to a violent storm that broke over their fields, she asked him, among other things, about his old love affairs. The request was so natural that he didn't even realize how very natural it was. That evening they talked to each other at great length; and when the maid knocked to bring them light, she was told to return later.

For all that, however, she never became a personage; nor a legend, which is so easy to do in the country. She was ever lively, understanding, and spirited. So sharp, in fact, that she understood perfectly well that in their behavior there was a touch of selfishness, and that the hostility and antipathy of the people around them was therefore reasonable.

But two days came whose effect, for a time at least, brought her back into touch with the world—despite the fact that she managed, in short order, to make those days "hers": the day on which the general, together with his Scottie, left for a colonial war; and the day, seven months later, when she was apprised of his death.

It was, I recall, in September, and the newspapers announced the event in two lines.

But we learned of it only much later, accidentally, and via a misplaced vowel.

It was (sometimes banality is inevitable) a terrible blow: the more so because she found it unjust, monstruous, and alien to her natural order. "Oh my God," she would say, twisting handkerchief or glove, "why did this have to happen to me, to me? It's different for other people. . . . Yes it is, different, very different." "There's no comparison," she added impatiently, as though overcoming some inner objection. "Don't people forget? Don't they forget a little more every day?" And she named names; and thought that in this, above all else, people were all alike. Nor were moments lacking in which she was convinced that she was being persecuted by something more intelligent and personal than fate itself. She tried doing ill, then doing good, but both brought her poor returns, and if finally she settled on doing only good it was because, after all, that was a lot easier.

She managed that for a few consecutive months. That is, until March. Then, occasionally, she was again seen out and about. She made the odd unnecessary purchase; sometimes she spoke briefly with someone. It was during this period that she began to keep a diary. "Ah, I'm no longer the same woman. I've become so good," she wrote a few days later, "that I now manage to look with a good heart on the happiness of others close to me. I am no longer offended. Is this possible? I don't even feel envy. . . ." And then, four pages later: "I am seriously worried. I really don't know what to do: I could give away half of myself. . . ." And more of the same.

She was indeed disposed to yield half of her all: but certainly not to accept the other half that people necessarily wanted to give her in return. She soon had to realize that her gift could never be accepted unless she, in turn, accepted her reward. This was asking too much from her. To tell the truth, it was beyond her strength.

Furthermore, her peasants no longer showed the respect they had in the old days; they looked at her with a certain expression, as though she had some obscure guilt. For instance, the way in which she smiled at certain things, and at problems by which they swore; the way she was serene and distant, and offered them, fundamentally, little more than maternal irony, perhaps that of her own presence. "The general, well, he understood," she almost felt them thinking. "He realized that he had no time left. . . . He went away just in time. . . . He understood. . . . But as for her, what's she waiting for?"

Thus it came about that she reduced herself to spending all her time in the house; and, because the grounds included an old chapel which she undertook to restore, she no longer went out even to go to church. This little island was, in fact, her definitive salvation and, little by little, the general's death was slowly transmuted into a bearable unhappiness—into, I can only guess, a sort of eternal evening. She might not have withstood a further shock; certainly she wouldn't have survived the extinction of her unhappiness. It was an unhappiness that she had constructed day by day, as others build, day by day, their own illusions. In its own way, that unhappiness was an illusion too: as to the past and as to the future. Yet it was absolutely necessary to her; it was, in fact, her self. The villa now constantly spoke of the general and what he had, in his day, meant to her: the old ways, serenity, good manners, and more. But she took marvelous care to avoid anything or anyone who could bring back to life, or make vivid, those memories. Had this happened, grief would again have supplanted this gentle unhappiness of hers, and that she did not want. For instance, she refused to go to a memorial service for the general; nor would she read a speech that recalled his death. One day, certainly, those two events would have become memories, and she would have discovered them bit by bit. Now, however, they were part of life; they spoke of a day barely past; and life was too much for her.

However, when she learned that a lady found herself in the area, a lady of whom many years before it had been said that she was an old flame of the general's, she did not fail to invite her to visit. It must have been a strange encounter: highly refined, serious, and at the same time faintly ridiculous, with the kind of absurdity that makes everything human. That day they, too, spoke at length. They spoke until, beyond the windows, the garden took on a certain violet tinge. Then, somewhat surprised, her visitor rose. At that point she was able to make out, beyond the ploughed fields and the vineyards, fleeting trails of smoke.

"Ah, his old ducks," she said suddenly, looking out on that rural squalor. She said it with a smile, as someone looking at an old childhood portrait discovers in that image the little defects of a person to whom one wishes well.

"What's that? You mean to say even 'then' he went hunting?" asked Signora Nodier, she too coming to the windows. And looked at her with a smile, for her visitor too was a little failing of the general's.

"Yes, but a dreadful hunter, then," her visitor said, laughing. "Not everyone wanted him around. They even found excuses to avoid him. Once they went so far as to invite him on the wrong day. . . . Luckily, he never found out."

"He never confessed as much to me," Signora Nodier brought out, after briefly consulting her memories. "But I think I always suspected that was the case." And she added, as if to herself, "He took it too seriously to be good at it."

"Almost solemnly," her visitor added.

"True, true," agreed Signora Nodier, almost grateful for a conclusion that made the general come alive. "Absolutely true, solemn."

And the pair of them began to talk of his defects: in such a way that they didn't seem to be speaking of one who was dead or alive, but of a myth, of the presence of one who combined a little of each, of life and death. Neither did either of them realize that the death, as well as other even sadder events, had taken place barely half a year earlier.

Signora Nodier considered that day one of the most important, and most "hers."

She was to know another such, and more important still.

One evening two years later, as the oldest of the maids was ironing, there was a ring at the gate. Against the garden lamp one could see snowflakes falling, and in between, rain. It was deep winter. After looking out the window, she said, turning to the young maid, "You go, Agata," and returned to her ironing.

She had to get up a few moments later, however, for though panting from her run across the garden, and though her feet were wet and a few flakes of snow clung to her hair, Agata reappeared smiling and excited, chattering about someone who stood outside the door. Then a soldier came in. Then a dog. The old woman immediately recognized the dog as the general's Scottie.

The soldier stood there looking around, bewildered. He knew nothing: only that, thanks to an old dog he'd never seen before, handed over to him by another soldier, he'd had to take a huge detour; that he was tired, it was raining, and his feet were wet. He found the whole thing exceedingly strange.

He found it even stranger when the young maid returned more than a half-hour later to tell him that her mistress thanked him profusely, found his gesture in bringing back the dog splendid, but on that evening couldn't possibly receive him—"in no way could receive him"—and accompanied him back to the gate.

"Giovanna," she said on her return, "I'm taking the dog over to the farmhouse."

"In this weather?" the old woman said, startled. "Can't he sleep next to the fire? And what if 'she' wants to see him? Is she supposed to go over there?"

"No, not in the house. Not here," the young maid said, standing with the dog at the open door. Outside you could still see snow and rain, and a row of dripping hedges. She looked for something to put over her head, but found nothing better than an old newspaper, which she took, and left. From the top step she turned once more to the old woman. "Be ready," she said. "She'll call you to give you a note."

But no note came from Signora Nodier the whole of the next day. Nor the day after. She stayed in her room, and the only time she came down was to ask the gardener something. But on the third day the note was on the table, addressed to Quintilio, the oldest of the peasants on her land.

I had access to it only many years later.

My dear Quintilio,

You won't mind, after so many years in which we haven't seen each other, if I ask you to do me a last favor? It's a big favor, but it is the last I will ask. You can be sure of that. I beg you above all, if you come, not to question me; don't ask me twice to explain myself, as if you hadn't understood the first time. The stranger this request seems to you, the better you'll have understood. But how silly I am! You're doing me a favor (you'll do it, won't you, Quintilio?) and it is I who impose

conditions. I really no longer understand myself. With friendly greet-
ings, to you, to old Maria, to the old Tromps, and to the old Felicità.
All old, now. How sad!

There was a postscript: "Don't refuse me this favor,
Quintilio. If for some reason you think you can't do me
this favor, do it for the little girl you once taught to fish."

The old peasant accepted on the spot.

A week later, I happened to be passing nearby and
paid her a visit.

As always, she received me well, and I had the impression that my conversation was not displeasing to her. I
remember that at one point she rose and left me alone for
a moment, so I was able to look around the room. To do
that in her presence would have struck me as offensive.

Thus I could see paintings, portraits, a few sticks of
queer furniture, a few old magazines, and an infinity of
tasteful objects: the whole of it looking like someone who
suddenly, of her own free will, without dying, has
stopped. Last, because it was partly hidden in the shadow
of a curtain, I saw the embalmed figure of a little Scottie
dog. This, too, I remember as partaking of myth, but also
of the present—somewhat more than a memory, almost a
pale memory.

Then she came back, apologized, and began to talk
again. From time to time I picked up noises from the road,
and I kept my eyes fixed on her; strange as it may sound,
she seemed nearly happy.

This is a true story.

THE OLD COUPLE

Whether it's from an excess or
a lack of sensibility, I don't know, but it's a fact that great
tragedies leave me indifferent. There are subtle pains, some
situations and relationships, that move me more than a city
destroyed by fire.

That is the first reason why I take up the story of the
two old Grimaldis.

They were born in a relatively happy time—around
1880, I believe—and for many years they were happy.
They enjoyed a comfortable income, and it is said that
both of them were very handsome people. Then things
changed.

In their fifties (after they had been living a somewhat
secluded life for better than ten years) their only son died.
If happiness had made them like hundreds of others, this
first loss made them strikingly different. It was from that
moment on that they truly became themselves. They no
longer went out; they hardly ever received. From fifty to
sixty (including the last four years of war) they became
increasingly aware that the well-being of a time gone by

was being implacably weakened, but they moved not a finger to prevent it. For ten years they merely observed, as one looks at the last curling ember of a letter being slowly consumed by fire in the chimney.

By then they were reduced to a single house. With a rather touching form of cynicism, they calculated the likely number of years remaining to them and weighed that against the sum they might receive from the sale. They decided to sell. Thus, having realized half, or even less, of what anyone else might easily have obtained, they retired to an apartment in the center of town. Or, as he said, who from his past had preserved only a baggage of maxims and paradoxes, "If you like, nothing could be farther from the center."

Thus began the third stage of their life, with neither of them suspecting that there would soon be a fourth stage. As a sort of ultimate coquetry, he set himself to reading Horace, while, pretending that it was indispensable, she did some light work around the house. In that way, the afternoons passed, and if in this world there are different kinds of happiness, I have no reason to doubt that they were nearly happy.

It happened, suddenly, on a Wednesday.

The clock in the nearby square was sounding half past ten and, as usual, the woman who came every day to clean and do the shopping took off her apron, said goodbye, and left in a hurry; before one o'clock she still had two other houses to do. But she returned immediately.

"There's a . . . gentleman asking after you," she said somewhat roughly, annoyed by the interruption. Signora Grimaldi looked around to see if everything was in order.

"I think we can manage to receive him here," she decided. "Show him in please, Maria."

Almost immediately, Maria returned. "I'm sorry, but he insists on speaking personally to *you*." Signor Grimaldi raised his eyes from his book.

"A young man?" he asked, turning to look at the maid.

"Yes," she answered, without grasping quite why she was asked. "Yes, definitely a young man. Barely thirty."

"Happy days, happy days," Signor Grimaldi said, shaking his head at his wife. "If you're in a hurry, don't wait for your husband to go out."

"I'd have a long wait if I did that," she answered, laughing. "It's been two years since you left the house."

Their age and their condition were now such that a visit was something of an event, an adventure; and never had there been any visits from young people. But now someone, someone young, was asking after her, personally. She couldn't quite understand why.

"It doesn't matter, it doesn't matter. Why apologize? Have I asked you anything?" he continued, bantering in the same tone. "I was reading Horace and didn't hear a word. Don't get all upset."

Smiling, Signora Grimaldi left the room. In the neighboring drawing room she found a young man of thirty or somewhat less, whom, naturally, she had never seen in her life, and whose name was totally unknown to her. He had a three- or four-day-old beard and wore an old yellow raincoat of the kind worn some years back by cavalry officers. Neither tie nor shoes showed any pretension beyond that of responding to necessity. In short, apart from a certain aggressivity in his manner, which was not especially off-putting, he was a typical poor literature student, destined to become a journalist but for the time being willing to give private lessons at a most reasonable price.

After both had sat down, he began with a kind of unconstrained and impatient cumbersomeness, at which he himself smiled, saying, "Well you see, it's like this, really. . . . The story is a bit long, I know that. But I don't think it can be cut by much. Well, I'm twenty-six, I'll be twenty-seven in August, and I'm a law student; or rather I'm registered for a year, and that's likely to be all. . . ."

"Like my son," Signora Grimaldi commented, who had decided to hear the young man out with maternal and flirtatious irony.

"I did a couple of years in Bologna. You know how it is. And another couple of years in Milan."

"Just like my son," she repeated.

"*Beh*," the young man shrugged with a smile, a little embarrassed at this unexpected coupling. "I imagine those are the only things we have in common. So, as I was saying," he continued, pointing to his raincoat and shoes, and perhaps to another form of wretchedness even deeper and more personal to him than these colorless garments, "I can't believe that he's not better off than I am."

Signora Grimaldi changed her tone.

"I wish I could be that certain. . . ."

"Oh, I'm so sorry," he said, somehow divining that her son must be dead. "I'm sorry. But even so, I think I must stand by my opinion."

And he waited with composed impatience for the wave of emotion raised in her by this allusion to subside so that he could continue his statement.

"Well," he began again after a few seconds, "if I were a little more coherent, even a little, nothing that you could think of me would matter in the least. But instead, I think I can say that you have some little esteem for me. Most stupid of me, isn't it?" (She said nothing.) "A few days ago, thinking ahead to our meeting, I had imagined a flow of fine words. True words, of course. For instance, that a man is always better than the things he says, and often better than the way he acts. Or something of the sort. But being here is different. Here. . . ."

He pulled his armchair a little closer to hers, for with his last words she had begun to listen to him, not exactly more attentively, but with a different sort of attention.

"Here I only want to say the following. I'm twenty-seven, I've worked, I've studied, I've kept myself busy. Besides which, I did two years in the war. I've done everything I could do, and sometimes things that I couldn't do, I assure you," he added, raising his voice as though she'd objected or her face had revealed some sort of disapproval. "I know that when one has a house like this, and armchairs like these, it's easy to look down on others."

"But I don't look down on anyone," she said quickly. "I've reached an age at which I think I manage even not to look down on myself—"

"All the better. That's what I was hoping for. It will make this easier for both of us," the student interrupted. "I haven't managed to finish anything. And if I go on this way, I'll manage to finish even less."

"Even less?" she asked, astonished.

"Yes, even less. For some people, 'nothing' is already something. But right now, better we should consider the two of us. Right. I'm about to do something that could be an infamous thing to do. Yes, other people would not hesitate to use the word 'infamous.'"

Instinctively, she raised her eyes and looked at him.

"Something infamous?" she asked.

"Ye—ess. Something infamous," he asserted, slowly and unhappily studying the toes of his shoes. "But take care, for I didn't lift a finger to discover it; and even if it had been the easiest thing in the world, I wouldn't have lifted a finger. I don't claim any great merit on my part, but it's the truth, so I tell you. But in fact the . . . yes, the infamy offered itself to me, of its own accord. It sought me out. I swear. It found my name, where I lived, my room; it came to me. No more, no less. And that being the case, that changes things, I think. You have to admit that. Things like that come from God knows where; one could in fact think they come from on high . . . from on very high. Who knows?"

Naturally, she (having always thought that infamy could only come from the lowest part of our natures) could not admit that an infamy should come from on high; at most she could allow that others might fall for something of the sort. The truth is that by now she was too upset to judge or reflect.

The young man continued: "Each of us has his touch of providence. And for an unbeliever like me I can't think of a better one than this. I mean to say that I don't think I have any right to look this gift horse in the mouth."

"Well then, speak up!" she said agitatedly. "What more do you expect?"

"All right," the young man concluded, "but first I had to tell you that, to convince you that I couldn't do otherwise."

"But what on earth do you care about convincing me? About what?"

The young man extracted a letter from his pocket and put it on the little table between them.

"This, Signora, is a letter that I think should interest you greatly; and one that moreover now interests me. When, along with other furniture of yours, you sold a desk, I found some forty letters like this in the third drawer on the left. Didn't I tell you that fate sought me out? Right, so what I want to say is that the third party to whom these letters would be even more interesting than to us is . . . is your husband. I know perfectly well that the one person who should not read these letters is your husband, and that you will do everything in your power to see to it that he continues to believe that no such letters were ever written. I also know that this very week you have sold a house and received a fair sum for it. Another might have made more from the sale than you, but the money you received is really quite sufficient."

Signora Grimaldi was beginning to grasp the young man's meaning and was about to reply. But he interrupted, and rushed to his conclusion.

"I think that one hundred fifty thousand lire ought to resolve the matter for all three of us. For the truth is, three of us are now concerned."

Once again she tried to say something; again he interrupted.

Standing up, he said: "No. Don't say a word. I know beforehand everything you might want to say to me; I've known for some days; and I think I agree with you. Yes, I agree with you. But that doesn't change a thing. Even as to the sum to be paid, there's nothing to be said: I could have asked for more, I could have asked for less. Instead, I ask

for just what I need, so that I no longer require such prov-
idential interventions."

There was a moment of silence.

"Today is Wednesday," he began again. "Saturday
morning at ten or eleven, or even later, if that suits you
better, I'll return with all the other letters."

She stood up as well, and followed him slowly to the
door. There the young man stopped briefly to study a portrait on the wall.

"There, you see," he said in a gentler voice, "my contacts with 'him' never added up to more than a couple of
years at university."

"He," she answered with melancholy irony, "was not
visited by this providence." He left.

"Now, now," her husband said, at that moment enter-
ing the drawing room with an open book in his hand and
seeing her. "Why this dark look now that you've got rid of
him?"

"Dear God," was all she felt like saying, "what a dreadful tie!" And she tried to fix the knot.

"Now, now, that's a bad sign. Anna Karenina realized
she no longer loved her husband when she saw what ugly
ears he had," he continued to joke.

"But at least you can change your tie," she replied, trying to adopt the same tone.

But she did not succeed. Nor did she succeed in smiling.

Only later, when she had read the letter, did it dawn
on her what that twenty-minute visit had really been for
her. Neither more nor less than this: ruin. Everything had
taken place in such a strange and unexpected manner, and

the tone of the meeting had been, up to the very end, so familiar that she had not been able to take in the disaster. And for that matter, the events to which the letter referred were by now in so distant a past that they seemed to belong to another life, of which her present life could at most be a remembering witness.

Thirty years before, at a time when her husband was flying off to Livorno every month and committing discreet follies with a young woman, someone had fallen in love with her. The man in question, who had both intelligence and money, and was conscious of both, had written her beautiful letters—at a time, and in a context, in which these seemed perhaps more important than his fortune. She in turn had fallen in love with him and had promptly replied. Nothing else. Nothing else had happened. And now that man was dead, and she was just an old woman who no longer even remembered the name of the man who had sent her that bundle of beautiful letters. The only element to which time had not brought both distance and innocence was the letter itself. That was the present; it was a living sin. Preserved by an ironical miracle, it was a stone from thirty years ago that fell suddenly into the lonely waters of their old age.

"Dear God," the Signora said, rising and shaking her head, "even the money's too much. Too much, far too much. And I'd have to lay my hands on it without his realizing anything. . . ." She was too desperate to be distressed by a lie but too tired to resort to one. She started listening to the rain outside.

Just then it began truly to pelt down hard, and her husband wasn't even able to help her lower the blinds before the rain turned into a storm. Both of them got thoroughly wet. Then suddenly the lights went out. Down below in the street they heard shouts and laughter.

Then they sat down side by side.

After a while, he said, "I don't think it was such a brilliant idea to sell the house." Although irony was his chief form of self-defense, and he had frequent recourse to it, now, what with the time of day, the darkness, and the rain, irony was useless.

"Oh, we won't live forever," she answered, guessing at his meaning.

"That's not what I meant," he lied.

"But I did," she said, some bitter mingling with the sweet. "That's just what I meant."

"It's all the rain's fault," he replied. "But I think we have no right to complain, not to mention the fact that it would be in poor taste. We knew how to be young when we were young, and now we know how to be old: I don't know many people who can say as much. There's something else I want to tell you. When Riccardo died, I thought there could be no greater injustice; I thought it was against the natural order. But now I think his death was part of a certain order. I may not understand it, but I'm sure it exists. . . . And much as I mourn him, I think that had he been alive he wouldn't have made our lives as united as they are. I think he too contributed to this masterpiece of ours. Seriously."

She remained silent.

After a long pause, she murmured, "These are things one says in the dark."

"Of course, of course. You need a little dark to say such things. And since the power's not back on yet, I have something else to say: the life of two old people is a thousand times more valuable than that of two young people. A thousand times. There's no comparing."

"It could be. I don't say no. But I've never heard anyone say that."

"That's because no one listens to us," he said. "And because by now we have enough sense to know it doesn't matter one iota whether others believe us or not."

"Yes, I too think that a little darkness is sometimes necessary," she admitted hesitantly. "So now I too want to tell you something. I think it's important to you and to me, and in light of what you said earlier . . . important."

He leaned back in his armchair; she drew closer to him. At that moment the lights came back on.

"I also think it wasn't so smart to have sold the house" was all she said. For that night, there was nothing more to be said. Both of them stood up.

Later, however, she waited until her husband was in bed before writing what follows:

My dear,

What you said today when the power went out is the truest thing I've ever heard you say to me, and I'd almost like to thank the storm that made it possible. I too wanted to tell you something, and I was about to open my mouth when the lights came back on. The result is I'm reduced to writing you a letter. It's a quarter to one, and you've been asleep for an hour.

You are about to read a letter that will pain you deeply; it will give you all the pain that, at our age, we are capable of experiencing. And Saturday morning, sometime around nine or ten, the young man who came to see me today, and about whom you joked a bit, will bring you a whole bundle of such letters.

I could have spared you this pain by paying the young man 150,000 lire, a third of what we obtained by selling our wretched little house. Had I done so, you would have been able to continue thinking that our life truly was the kind of masterpiece you described, and that with his death our Riccardo contributed to it. But now think about it. Think about your pain and mine, think about the melancholy and coldness we'll feel to the end of our days. And all for want of a miserable sum that our old steward could have made in a fortnight or less. How little we're worth! Any young person would be offended by so little, and I'm not sure I'd say he was wrong. But you and I, my poor Enrico, are past sixty, and we're alone in the world. Today I had to convince myself that being happy or thinking oneself happy is a luxury we can no longer afford—no more than we can our former dignity, our pride, and so much else. We have three or four years left to live. Perhaps, God spare us, five. And it occurred to me that there remains only one duty for us: to be able to await, day by day, our end.

I know full well that your greatest bitterness will not be from the pain the letter will cause you, but from the realization that your happiness has been sold at such a cheap price—for much less than what those presents cost that you gave me in the past, not thinking that they were anything but trifles.

All of this is sad, my poor Enrico. All this is so sad that I can find no word of hope or apology. It's two and you're still asleep. You're breathing a little heavily. And you don't know anything yet.

Giovanna.

A MOMENT OF THIS SORT

"Eh, Turkish times, Turkish times. . . ."

You don't expect much from a schoolteacher, I know that; but in that business I played the teacher part to the full.

It was Saint Veronica's Eve and everyone was pouring out of farmhouse and yard into the country. People even came down along the paths through the fields from the hills, from four kilometers away and more. From behind hedges kids were playing fool games, wearing sheets, carrying pumpkins and lanterns to frighten the women. And in the middle, girls and music, firecrackers and laughter, and a Saturday night moon, the color of copper and rose, bigger than a basin.

"Here's a fine night," I thought; and as the book I had in my hand was about the plague in Athens, dead bodies on every page, I threw it aside and pressed my nose to the window that gave out onto the orchard and took off my glasses. "Yes, a delightful evening. And if I had a suit that fit and two shoes that matched, I too would party, with a girl or even two, and see the morning in."

Words. Just words. Because the suit was what it was,

so were the shoes and the rest of me; and that's the way it would always be, a nickel and dime sort of life.

So it was that, without so much as a tie, I slipped through the orchard on tiptoe, like someone stealing grapes, and headed for the road leading to the woods and the canal.

"So take what you've got in life," I said to myself. "A few fireworks and a bunch of frogs. No jackpot, that's for sure. But at least if I don't run into Cloanti, it'll be a decent evening."

Just then, Cloanti said, "How's things?" He was leaning against an old ash tree, whittling at a stick with his pocketknife. The moment he saw me he stepped out of the shadows. It was obvious he'd been there for some time, waiting for me.

"Schoolteacherish," I replied, not stopping, just talking.

"Not so good then," he laughed, walking alongside me.

We walked a bit in silence. I was already feeling sick.

"It looks like your neighbors are going to make a fine racket tonight," he said, cordial, and also impudent. "Some widow's remarried?"

"No one's given me any confetti," I said. "And if I slipped out of the house, it's so I won't hear them. So I don't have to listen to anyone."

"In that case I have just the ticket. My neighbors never open their mouths." He laughed. His laugh was both stupid and not stupid. No one could have said what was going on in his mind. "You want one or two neighbors like that, you can have them, at cost."

It was a strange way of talking, and I couldn't help glancing at him. This Cloanti was a squalid little man. He

had a field and a vineyard at the top of the hills, and he
knew no one, because he'd only arrived recently. He was
too smart for a peasant and not smart enough for anything
else, besides which, like all the widowers out there in the
deep country, there was something equivocal about him.
He had two clear blue eyes, which in a child would have
been angelic but on him were plainly just obscene; plus a
whole lot of other little things that made me look for the
exit whenever he popped up. Only for three or four days
now he'd been paying me court, with a raft of compliments and *bonjours;* his talk was all of education and culture
and how badly the government treated us teachers; and
once, thinking it would please me, he got onto patriotism.
A con man, that's what he was. A hundred and thirty
pounds of cunning and lowlife, not including his head.

"Sir," he said falteringly at one point.

We had reached a crossroad, and one part of it leads
up the hill. The moon brightened the willows. Nearby, in
the reeds, a frog had started singing. Farther away, below,
lights shone; the noise and the firecrackers and the music
reached us as when a thunderstorm splashes the road and
one runs to shut the windows. There was nobody at all on
the road.

"Sir," he repeated. He stopped and spoke in a quite
different tone of voice, "What I was saying a while back,
that was all foolishness, that's all, like when you're talking
to a woman and you have to make a start somewhere. Just
like the clink of coins. . . . Or not even a clink. . . . You're
alone; me too. And we come from someplace else. We're
birds of passage, we are, and everyone looks at us. For the
time being they don't talk to us. But they're ready enough
to jump on us if we poke our noses into their affairs."

All this preamble was much too polite for somebody as ill put together as he, and it didn't fit at all. When someone starts talking like that, all you get out of it is being touched for a loan, a gift, a subscription to an encyclopedia, or a scheme that's going to cost you plenty.

"If that's the way it is, then we're better off minding our own business," I said.

"A good rule," he answered. "Rule Number One, I know that," he admitted with a kind of sweeping gesture. "But what if your business is already someone else's business? Have a look here."

It was one of the metal buckles the German soldiers wore on their belts.

"For the last three months, every kid in the area has had one," I said, barely glancing at it. "They play soldier."

"Yes," he said patiently, taking his buckle back. The worst of it was that he seemed calmly and unworthily ready to accept all my insolences and insults to the end of his days, and mine. "Right. Every kid around has got one or two of them. And they play at soldiers and have a world of fun. But say you were digging around your vines and found one of these just a few inches underground. You tell me, sir, would you want to play with it? (Age aside, of course.)"

I stopped without even wanting to.

"And on top of the buckle, bits of cloth . . ."

I kept my mouth shut.

"And a leather strap . . . black . . . like the brigadiers wore round here, looking for partisans."

I raised my eyes and looked at him.

"That's right," he said. "Four days ago. In my field."

He took my elbow. "We can be there in a matter of

minutes. . . . You can see the place from here . . . it's a few hundred yards. . . ."

I shook myself free.

"No thank you. . . . Don't even think about it. We don't have any business together. Why don't you go talk to the priest? That's definitely his line of business."

"I thought about that. Three days and three nights I thought about it, and I was on the point of going. But priests aren't what they used to be. They've become something like lawyers. You're a different matter."

He looked down at his shoes, like someone who's turned up a pretty good card but has an even better one up his sleeve.

"I'm sorry, I really am, Cloanti. But try and understand me, too," I answered, also changing my tone of voice. "I'm twenty-four years old, I've read a lot of books, my eyesight's failing and here I am. Look at me. Look at my shoes, look at my clothes. What's underneath is even less good, take my word for it. Take into account that's the way it always going to be. It's worse than purgatory. But when I think of my old friends, the old all-night party kings who if they want to go out now at nights have to grow a beard, the others, here and there, who've all finished going to the devil. . . . Well, my friend, I'm attached to my own bones and I don't even think of asking for a penny more. This is an ugly tale, I know, but thank God it's not mine: so I close my eyes and ears and wait for the whole thing to blow over. I'm sorry, but from a substitute teacher up in the hills you can't expect any better."

"You're right," answered Cloanti abstractly. "Yes, you're right. I was talking nonsense, and I knew what you'd say—the more so because we don't really know each other very well, and we're a pair of bed-and-board types, you and I. . . . And then it's my business, really. You were quite right. Yes indeed. Tied to duty. Goodnight, sir."

"*Beh*, that's stupid of you, Cloanti. Just hang on. They're not exactly going to run away, are they? And this business of being just boarders here: you know perfectly well that means nothing at all. The fact is, these are curious times, and they shoot even kids. You know that. Don't pretend you're deaf. As far as I'm concerned, my career, girls, a decent place to live, and all the rest don't matter: all I want is peace and quiet. I want peace, that's all. I'd like to live to be an old man."

"No, no, you're right. I understand," the ignoble little man said, ignoring me completely. "How could I not? I don't know you, I haven't spent my life with books, and suddenly I jump up out of nowhere and say, 'Come with me!' Oh thank you so much, kind sir, that's a bit too quick and easy. Just like a woman! . . . It's my business, as you say, just mine, so don't get involved: to a meal of that kind, one doesn't invite a fine fellow like you to sit down! Goodnight, sir."

He put such undignified humility and understanding into his speech that my hands began to itch.

"Well, if that's the way you want it, goodnight to you too," I said angrily.

But that Rigoletto had the guts to turn around again. Now he seemed nobly disdainful.

"No sir. Not just like that. I know I haven't sweated over books, and I never went to school; but you who've studied, you shouldn't talk to me like that. It's not right for someone like you. You know there are no ordinary nights for the likes of me. You know that, you people. You say, I won't come; 'nothing you have to say counts,' you people say. I've never poked my nose in your business: and that's all right; and I know I spoke stupidly, and amen to that. And thanks for the lesson. But to make fun of me, sir . . . when I've got no book-learning, and it can't be any fun for you. Goodnight."

He started climbing away, alone, between two hedgerows, and I stood there in the middle of the road looking after that bagful of gross malice and calculation, imprudence and wretchedness, with less shame than a cat.

Six paces later, he turned around.

"No hard feelings, sir," he said, as if throwing me a tip.

In two long strides I caught up with him. I'd happily have torn his hair out.

"You want to know something, Cloanti?" I said calmly. "Ten years ago I saw a circus with horses and a tall clown with a funny cap on and a red nose, and his face whitened with chalk. . . ."

"I've seen the like. When I still had my wife I went, and more than once. I only like the man on the high wire."

"That's not what I'm talking about. I just want you to know that man in his funny cap was worth ten of you."

"Watch out for the ditch, sir," he said apprehensively. He was such a lowlife that in his way he was invulnerable.

We got there.

He didn't want to look me in the eye, so beckoned that I should crawl through the hedge, the thorns of which he held apart with all the grace of a high-class waiter; then, once we were in the field, he went ahead, and from a corner where he had them ready, produced a pick, a hoe, and a couple of spades, which he carefully placed at my feet as though laying out a picnic. "Maybe it's all a fantasy," he said, looking around. "Though once, I have to tell you, I found a shoe."

In reply, I struck the ground with the hoe. He got to work himself.

We put in two or three hours without addressing a word to each other, without even looking at each other, he on one side, myself on the other; and with every shovelful I thought of that obscene loner's look he had, and of my being so stupid as to talk to him the way a woman does to a priest. With every stroke I dug deeper and with greater anger, and it didn't even feel like work.

Another half-hour went by.

At a certain point, he said, "Sir. . . ." I didn't even turn round. "Sir," he repeated, and I no longer heard the sound of the spade. Then a third time, after a long pause: "Look . . . Look, Jesus!"

And then finally I turned around. And what there was to see, I saw.

Oh, it's easy enough to say. It's different being there.

We stayed there for a while by the pit, silent. Then, hardly looking at each other, in a measured way, we began to refill the hole.

"I suppose it mustn't matter that much to them," he muttered through his teeth. "You agree?"

I nodded. "One place is as good as another for them. Their day's done."

"In Lent," he said.

We continued to pile the earth back in. When we'd finished and we could no longer see those four faces, and the hands and feet finally vanished, the lights had long gone out and no sound reached us from down below. The girls had all gone home laughing some time ago, and even the frogs were silent. The moon was right above us, and I'd never seen it so cold and pale and distant.

Slowly we picked up the spades and the rest.

"Turkish times, Turkish times," Cloanti commented; and then, "Tomorrow I'll plant a few cherry trees."

It was cold, and I was sweating. I put on my jacket.

"Willows might be quicker," he said, half out loud. "There's nothing to understand, right? That way, no one will know a thing."

I nodded again. "It'll all be just as before," I said. "All you need is a green thumb."

"All through the summer there was someone making love up there."

"They'll come back," I said, "and the willows will make it that much nicer for them."

That made him thoughtful. He approached me again.

"It's getting to be daylight," he said. "In a half-hour the carts will start going by. Somebody could come by. How about coming in for a glass of wine to warm you up?"

I shrugged without looking at him. "A fine Saint Veronica's Night, thanks a lot," I said. I pushed through the hedge hastily, scratching my neck and hands; then, with my collar turned up, I set off down the hill.

The moon was now the color of zinc and barely visible. There were bits of silver paper, orange peel, and trampled flowers all along the road. Between the hill and the ends of the valley, no one, not a dog, not a toad or any other living creature stirred. Nary a starling in the air. And everything the color of stone. To my left, far away, a dawn was rising, the color of dirty snow: an hour at which, in the bends of the roads and on windows, along with dead insects and all the beasts distractedly killed in the dark, and the garbage and mess, the gray collects its full freight of infamy, indifference, weariness, and despair of the compromises and forgotten matters of a day in the life of the world.

Halfway down the hill, I had to turn around; I *had* to, I tell you.

"Ho there, Cloanti!" I shouted from down below, waving my arm up at him. "I don't drink, you understand? I can't accept your invitation. Beer, maybe beer; but not wine. But thanks all the same."

In fact he was still standing there behind the hedge, outlined against that zinc-colored sky—like some poor harmless devil left behind by a barbarian army which, having destroyed everything in sight, had judged him to be unworthy of death, and condemned him, among those ruins, to be no more than a scarecrow.

Finally he smiled and nodded. He too waved his hand.

"If that's the way it is, I'll get you some beer tomorrow!" he shouted. "German beer. Special beer."

"Tomorrow then," I shouted. "But get inside; this dawn air's treacherous."

"You too. Get to bed. . . . No school tomorrow, sir. Pay attention to me, even if I'm stupid."

Yes, I understood. And he too had understood.

I didn't go. And three days later, when I saw him again, thirty yards away and wearing that same obscene look on his face, I still wanted to vanish, and headed up the first alley I could find. And the next day. And still today, when better than three years have gone by, if not more. I foresee it will always be like this, until the day when, after a peasant fair, we two friends who've witnessed a world without pity, memory, or hope, no longer run across each other in a dawn the color of dirty snow.

This is all a little ridiculous, isn't it?

OUR MONDAY, A PREFACE

As with all things in this
world, even this book has a kind of story. Perhaps the
main reason why everything has a right to a little respect
is that of having a story. Of course, I don't ask for respect:
I don't think I should ask anything for myself. To each his
own, and so on: that's all there is to it.

All things considered, I had whatever was coming to
me: I'm not about to stand in line for my turn. What I'm
trying to say is that in writing this novel I've had the best
two years of my life. The two "truest" years. I want to be
clear about this. Day by day I put in three eternal years of
war, then Egypt, then India. Something happened every
day: tents got erected and trenches dug, and eighty-kilo-
meter marches and more, and of course one killed and
died. Everything was immediate and concrete and logical
too: everything had a consequence and a purpose. An
Australian 88 fired and that meant a boat bridge blew up;
a K6 tanker appearing on the Tobruk-Bardia truck road
meant three-quarters of a liter for each man in the pla-
toon; and after all, nothing was "true."

Then I put in three years as a journalist. Every day except Sunday I explored police headquarters, hospital, town hall, court house, tax office and every possible venue for happenings. These were difficult times, the paper even more wretched, and above all I didn't want to lose my job. So I did everything I could to make the events I reported on as numerous and accurate as possible, and they were, too ("Bicycle Escapes" . . . "Wields Gun, Thinks It's Empty" . . . "Orgy on Trinity Road"). These stories, too, were anything but true. Basically, six false years. In fact, nothing is more of a lie than an isolated event. My two true years were 1949 and 1950 when I started to write this novel. Not just doing that, but by writing, hour by hour, others became true for me. I recaptured them. And words. I repeat, I don't ask for more. Nothing in the whole wide world is more beautiful than writing. Or painful. Or likely to make people laugh. Perhaps this is the only thing I know how to do.

As that's more or less the point I've reached, I'd like it if every man, having exercised every possibility in the world, would one day sit down and write a big novel (fine or not, it doesn't matter; that's his business, up to the stars); take a couple of years, or even three, or maybe a fair portion of his life. I'm serious; I have no intention of joking. It shouldn't cost anyone between thirty and forty too much pain to stop for a moment: to consider himself and others, too, and write a big novel with the greatest number of characters possible. In my view, that would be worth it. Ever so many things, I suppose, and perhaps even money, and love, the desire to succeed and icy disillusionment, would no longer be so obsessively important. It may be this is all perfectly clear, and doesn't need saying: perhaps not. Too bad. In any case, what matters is that I'm not joking or, worse, behaving peculiarly. Only things that are absolutely normal are, in fact, strange: strange enough to be frightening.

And here's my story.

I, too, realize perfectly well that I can't offer any excuses, but I'd like it if you'd believe me. I fear I'll never again be rid of this weakness: I like to be believed.

This is, so to speak, a prehistory. The real story will come out a bit later.

Twenty years ago, more or less, our city was as it is now in this regard: that a score of young men would get together every night in a café and say splendid things until two or three in the morning (or even four on Saturday nights)—bright as you could wish, with spirit, pride, good taste and modesty and everything else. And at heart, a certain innocence. We spoke, as is right, of literature.

What is curious is this: that we already read old Conrad, old Melville, and Chekhov: sometimes we greeted each other with a phrase from *Lord Jim* or "Bartleby," and we would have given our right arms, and more, to write a story like Chekhov. "How human, how human," we said; at a week's notice we were quite capable of organizing a meeting with the participation of some other local glories. That's the way it was: everything that emerged from us was that and nothing but that—a column, a half-column or less, shinier and colder than nickel. We talked about "informed" or "necessity" ("message" came later); we used the words "chaste," "remote," or "lunar" and other words even more abstemious; we dealt with children, dreams, and angels, or all three together, and a man with, so to speak, the head of a dog, when in fact he was neither man nor dog and spent all day up in his attic without ever opening his mouth, never doing much though, clearly, underneath, there was a deeper meaning, or maybe two, sometimes nothing at all. In practical terms we never managed to get a man to make two or three credible statements, but when it came to ghosts, children, and corpses, no one could do better than us. We were specialists in the matter. All we needed was a sheet and a tiny garden and a boy at dusk looking at the sheet and the garden, and something simply exquisite popped right out. The "lost generation" had already done what we all knew. And then there was Faulkner and Hemingway. And poor Wolfe, who'd already found his long way home. And the cinema. And lots of things.

And would you believe it, in the end they wound up taking us seriously. First a few magazines (we had copies for all of us, on handmade paper). And then some newspapers, too. And then all of them. Even some critics. They mistook us for young; we became a group, known as "the young," all of which was faintly comical. Some innocent and authoritative old man, at half-mast from times gone by, took us, who knows why, under his benevolent wing, and in his absolute simplicity never even suspected that there are times when no one is older than a young man. Or that we were, to say the least, two or three times older than he. And that's not funny at all.

The big-time publishers were more difficult.

Our important publishers, as a group, are a hard-nosed lot. They're both leathery and pliable; in fact, you never know what they're thinking. They know: oh yes, they know! But that's a story that could take us too far afield. With us they discovered this system. They wrote us very entertaining letters: in the first few lines they made it clear we were obviously ready to join the ranks of the most illustrious in this century; in the last two lines they revealed that the difficulty of the times obliged them to refuse our manuscripts. They blamed the public, etc. Above all, they were determined to show us a kind of polite disdain. We were wrong to be angry: those letters were worthy of us. And eventually we won out even there. And so on: to the Academy!

Then, in '40, the war.

Literature is the most complicated of all sicknesses: there is no known cure. Young writers are sometimes the most offensive of people. Every day I am convinced that to put up with them a man needs a good deal of spirit, just as the literati need a fair amount to put up with that sort of respect-disdain that will accompany them to the end of time. Who knows why? The world is a strange place.

In their innocence, young writers are led to believe that the world was made for them, not they for the world (which is exactly the contrary of those old men who consider themselves indispensable to the world when in fact the world has no idea what to do with them and flees them as if they were so many much-honored old maids. Never, ever, will you be able to convince them that after fifty indifference to the world is the best balm for intolerable ills. Never, ever, will they renounce their roles as incarnate reproaches or consciences or worse. On this point, too, each gets what he deserves.).

Thus a good number of us scorned the war, mainly because it upset all our former plans and gave us a sense of our own measure. When children play in the yard, the sudden appearance of a grown-up is always inopportune. But I don't want to be misunderstood: there are also very serious games.

Anyway, what a pity. Work so well contrived. A little garden so curry-combed and well-watered for four, five years and more: and now here's the war. Those modest people who saved their money so carefully, and were later caught by inflation, can have felt, as they waved their by-then worthless bonds in the air, no different from us. Only we literati showed ourselves infinitely more capable. We were truly great. We soon found ways to console ourselves. If the war gave us nothing else, it gave us a new set of sensations. Good. We would have put those in our books as well. Even an epic (the moon was nearer to us than that). Like all half-educated men, we were rather selfish, calculating, and a little bit vile. Perfect administrators of our little bit of earth.

Almost all of us went off. Whatever the sector, we were soon found to be pitifully inadequate, except as censors. But they used old men for that: us they sent to the front; me, to Croatia.

If I now talk a little about myself, it's only because it's convenient, and for no other reason: what happened to me at the time happened to almost everyone.

What's more, if one had wanted to write an adventure novel in those years, its hero would certainly have been a man who got up peacefully every morning at eight, ate his egg in milk, and wore a pretty good woolen jacket. Followed then the walk to the office. Followed a walk and a girl. Finally, coffee.

There were some. A few there were. I know some.

In three years of war we saw quite a bit. Snow all year: water under the bridge. I don't like talking about it. I swore I would never talk about it again.

But in Croatia, in Credavik and Musruk, fate thrust me upon the stage. Of course, I was the least likely man for the part: at best I was one of those uneasy talents forever snatching at beauty but never disposed to take a step in search of it. I liked looking, a lot. That's the whole story. I had this rather questionable gift of an above-average fantasy that allowed me to apply fresh varnish to even the most degrading or wretched sights, a slightly ignoble irony that enabled to me to laugh and smile at them, and a southern indolence that kept me from sinking into the very depths of boredom. When you come right down to it, I could appreciate the interesting more than the beautiful, and with all the originality at my command I felt the banal in all its complexity. Glance and comment were all I needed. No action. The fact is that by a slightly ironical circumstance I found myself in charge, and when one is at war, one cannot allow an Albanian shepherd to signal airplanes with his white and dappled goats. Everything went according to the rules: you could even say justice was done. But this too means less than nothing. He was, I think, a Muslim.

This was in Credavik. In Musruk, a Croatian student, a girl.

Then at El Medisah, I was taken prisoner.

Even now I would swear that Rommel was the finest general in the world. It's not true, as someone later said, that he had the brains of a quartermaster sergeant. He didn't need them; he was complete as he was: such a mind would have been out of place. Just to look at him we began to think of our own minds with some uneasiness, as if our brains were a little off, feminine, shameful. There wasn't a crack in the man through which any anxiety could enter. With him we were always safe. In Agedabia. In Suleim. Even against Ritchie's hundred-plus tanks. That day Rommel was a magnificent puppet-master and Ritchie broke his stick on him.

At El Alamein, too, we were perfectly safe with Rommel. Except that Alamein was the Deluge.

An hour after the attack it was all up with us: maybe even an hour earlier. Our company was suddenly surrounded and our guns no longer fired. From all sides we saw them advancing through the windblown sand, and for those of us still standing there was only one hope left, that these were the British. But the British wore ridiculous round helmets. Whereas all we saw through the sand was long, thievish locks: these were Freiberg's Australians. Difficult for anyone who was there on that day to forget them.

There, too, I saw a few things and swore I'd never talk about them again. The fact that three months earlier we'd done more or less the same thing to them served to give us some little self-esteem. Little, very little.

Of epics, or books, no one thought. I think we thought of nothing at all.

So, along with 4,200 other officers, I spent two years in Lahore, at the foot of the Himalayas.

Colonel Lawrence of Arabia coined a memorable phrase such as no one has had the luck to write in some years: to be dead in life.

My first six months were just that. Dead in life.

Leaning up against the barbed wire, hands in pockets, looking at a vast expanse of grain and the peaks of the Himalayas; and feeling time washing over us. The sunsets are unbearable. Indian sunsets are the most depressing and desolate in the world. There comes a moment when the flag-red breaks up into green, then lilac, then violet, and finally blue; the impression is that we're flaking off ourselves. Worse yet is when the west wind brings us fragrant waves of poppy. Not a few wept at dusk: openly, without shame, taking pity on themselves. Further, they were pretty polite with us, so we couldn't say anything. Then this too passed. We got used to this too. Sooner or later nearly all of us learned what one should learn at birth: that to any man anything may happen; crying or giving oneself airs is not our business.

Around December, the camp commandant allowed us to play a few games of tennis. As is often the case with the most obtuse measures, its success was totally unexpected.

Towards the end of '45 I returned. I was among the first. Thousands of others, in Lahore and Dacca, had to wait another year; those in Kenya, two.

After having regularly untuned a whole life, fortune finally noticed me; it came after me personally, a long way. It served only to make me suspect. But since there I was, it would perhaps have been better if we remained enemies. For the way it was, it seemed in a great hurry to pay off its debt; I now ought to consider myself even with fortune and I could no longer have any pretenses. Among the inconveniences of a somewhat miserable youth is that nothing dies harder or more degradingly than the feeling that if you find a worthless coin in the road you think it's more than you deserve. As in a Chaplin film, if the sun breaks through you suddenly feel a cop behind you. For children and women there may be nothing better: for a man, no; that's something else. Meanwhile, life belongs to others.

In September I was in Rome.

Ever beautiful: twice as beautiful in September. Towards evening, there's always a splendid sun such as there is only in Rome in September. There was expectation everywhere. Many people came back; others disappeared; the windows were full of people looking out on what was happening, or what might have happened below. As old Flaubert pointed out, a number of illustrious figures, professors, writers, members of two or three academies, even foreign academies, awaked to find themselves idiots for the rest of their lives, and no one thought to wear mourning for this fact: indeed, no one noticed. The Allies scurried about in jeeps from morn to night: as though they'd landed among us for no other reason. And from morn to night the Negroes were utterly drunk. On every corner you'd find them stretched out on the ground and surrounded by kids. The first bars reopened. Along the Via Veneto, with a Johnny Walker or a Black Label before them, appeared the young Hemingways, with chewing gum. Old movies arrived from America. Rear Admiral Ellery Stone got married. People began to read commentaries of commentaries on Marx. Diaries and memoirs by the dozens appeared. There were exhibitions of cubists, abstracts, intimists, realists. Once hermetic writers, authors of novellas, wasted not a day before issuing books four and five hundred pages long. Only the priests hurried about with heads lowered, hands tucked in their sleeves, like refined boarders, without so much as a grazing glance.

There was expectation everywhere. Everything was provisional, somewhat false and easy. It was all a spectacle.

Rome is not Milan. It is the least Roman city in the world. Micawber is Rome's true father. Under a sun of that sort, to go round and about in the streets was the finest thing in the world, for the moment; and for many of us, the only possible thing to do. Round and about with our hands in our pockets. Waiting. In this regard, '45 was a great year. I'd say we felt like convalescents. All we had to do was stand there with our hands in our pockets and wait, because it was all going to happen, soon. Besides, we had already paid for our tickets and we felt perfectly at ease. We were waiting for the curtain to rise. A few months went by, and nothing happened. We let a few more go by. The curtain never rose off the ground.

The wonder of it is, they sent us home without reimbursing us for our tickets.